SIX

THE SMOKE THAT THUNDERS

J.M. MANYANGA

A SIX THRILLER

Big Brains
PUBLISHING LLC

Published by Big Brains Publishing LLC
www.bigbrainspublishing.com

First Edition, January 2022
Paperback ISBN: 978-1-7367883-5-6
e-Book ISBN: 978-1-7367883-4-9

Publisher's Cataloging-in-Publication
(Provided by Cassidy Cataloguing Services, Inc.)

Names: Manyanga, J. M., author.
Title: The smoke that thunders / J. M. Manyanga.
Description: First edition. | [Saint Louis, Missouri] : Big Brains Publishing LLC, [2022] | Series: SIX series ; book 1.
Identifiers: ISBN: 978-1-7367883-5-6 (paperback) | 978-1-7367883-4-9 (e-Book) | 978-1-7367883-6-3 (audiobook) | LCCN: 2022901047
Subjects: LCSH: Espionage--Fiction. | Spies--Fiction. | Undercover operations--Fiction. | International crimes--Fiction. | Organized crime--Fiction. | Africa--Fiction. | LCGFT: Thrillers (Fiction) | Detective and mystery fiction. | Action and adventure fiction. | BISAC: FICTION / Mystery & Detective / International Crime & Mystery. | FICTION / Thrillers / Espionage. | FICTION / Thrillers / Crime. | FICTION / Thrillers / General.
Classification: LCC: PS3613.A5858 S591 2022 | DDC: 813.6--dc23

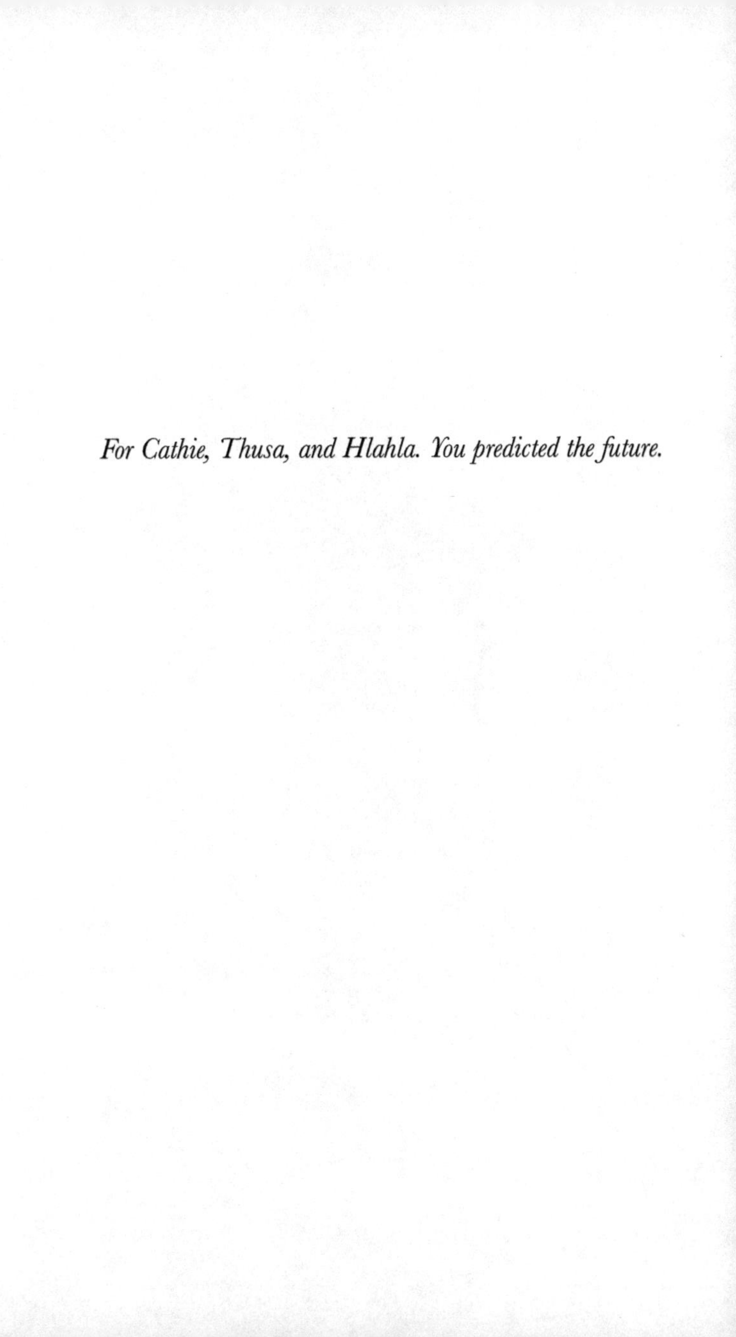

For Cathie, Thusa, and Hlahla. You predicted the future.

ACKNOWLEDGMENTS

I'm grateful for the continued support from my family; I couldn't have written this book without them.

Super thanks to countless people who continue to inspire me every day, intentionally or by chance.

THE SMOKE THAT THUNDERS

CHAPTER ONE

TO THEM, his name was Draye. His friends called him Six. A lone wolf. That's what his grandmother called him, asking when he was going to get married.

Six sprinted up the steep climb, over vines, dead logs, and shrubs. Never saw a snake, even in these dense rainforests in the Eastern Highlands of the country. While most of his compatriots preferred pumping stationary iron bars and weights in gyms, expensive gyms, loading up on steroids and protein powder, building masses of meat useless for real life, Six preferred the old way—the spartan way. He found this type of exercise more practical. Trial by fire. He enjoyed letting his body do the work—running the hills, climbing twenty-foot trees, swimming in treacherous rivers, ploughing the field, chopping firewood, and helping in the field when he could. Plenty of vitamin D from the sun. Robust immune system from all the bugs, mosquitoes, tsetse flies, mopane flies. Had only had a long bout of roundworm infection when he first visited. He thrived on whatever was available. Eating local, whatever was in season: insects, mopane worms, flying ants, termites, crickets, locusts, pumpkin leaves, blackjack, fish, bananas, sugarcane, mangoes, guavas, mice, warthogs, and occasional goat meat. Insulated from big food companies. This part of the country was immune from nutritional gurus and food experts, and the confusion that came with what, which, or when was the perfect diet. No wonder there were so many metabolic disease cases now. And a boom in the pharmaceutical world. Medicine and more medicine. Now these culprits were bringing the same poisonous food to the motherland. The locals liked it: pizza, cheeseburgers, fried chicken—it was good. TV stuff. Intentional. Of course. And people getting fat. So many chronic conditions. A perpetual whirlwind of eating junk, getting fat, buying workout programs, getting sick, then buying medicine for the rest of your life. The body was an adaptability machine. He understood the human body was malleable, not a mechanical system that can be fine-tuned by some specific diet. His physique was proof.

His stomach grumbled. *The boiled cow intestines!* he thought.

SIX STOOD at the top of the hill, looking at his chiseled, sweat-drenched arms. He controlled his breath, feeling the shortage of oxygen at that elevation. He felt the cool air warm in his lungs as he jogged higher and higher. It was beautiful. This place gave him some space and solitude from his life. It allowed him to meditate, reorient himself, and be at peace. He smiled at the thought of peace in his head. *There was no peace in his life. He killed people for a living,* he thought. *But, yeah. Bad people.* This hill was also the only place with a network; a crappy phone network. Roaming was expensive, and he preferred to use that money for gifts to people who needed them.

He liked to be here—his refuge. The fresh air, the trees, no humans, only nature. With days filled with exploration and relaxation—exploring wildlife, identifying birds, often by their calls, memorizing indigenous tree names, and had yet to see the revered pangolin. Here he would sit for hours, sometimes lie down enjoying the breeze. The locals believed the area was sacred and prohibited, which left the area all to himself. So far, the only close to scary thing he had encountered was a pair of mountain lions. He never hand-carried his pistol. No one would look for him here. He could be a ghost. To his grandparents and family here, he was the rainmaker from the U.S. He was the doctor. He had told them so. Google made it easier to suggest treatments when they asked.

He liked pain. A true product of the "no pain no gain" hype. With intense workouts filled with yelling expletives that seemed to push him higher. But since coming here, he had taken it easy several days a week, then went hard one or two days. This was one of those days. His level of fitness required less maintenance, especially as he wasn't pumping himself with sugar, fat, and salt—everything from the West. He found out that he ran faster, recovered faster, felt sharper, and slept better. Had inherited good genes that seemed to repel from his body the McChickens, soda by the liters, and cheap ramen noodles he had survived on in his college days. He had remained trim.

He watched two falcons shoot up and down, trapping a smaller bird. Brutal! He sat down in an asana posture, took a few deep, controlled diaphragm breaths, and closed his eyes. The rock surface felt stiff against his back.

The distinct ding shook him like a rock, interrupting the peaceful stillness up there forty feet above the ground on the massive granite hill. His reflexes reached for the pistol. Instinct. It was not there. He caught himself, hearing the incoming message beep on his phone. A distinct ringtone—one he knew very well. Only one person knew his local number. He took three deep breaths from his diaphragm, which moved up and down. He stretched and fetched the sixty-dollar phone from his cargo pocket. These words:

Vic Falls. 6:00 a.m. Tomorrow.

Just five brief words. That was enough. He knew what it all meant. His gut clenched. It always did, each time, no matter how many times he had done these missions.

He checked the timestamp. It had to be the same day because he had been up here the day before.

Six stretched some more and cracked his

shoulders, realizing the wind had picked up speed, and with it some cool air. *The higher you go, the cooler it becomes*, he thought. Cliché, but still true. He felt good. Meditation always did him good. His mind was clear. He needed that. Especially in his line of work. Many who did what he did for a living often resorted to drugs, cigarettes, reckless sex, alcohol, or something along those lines. But he had never been a fan of that. If he was going to die, he would die the right way, not by frying his liver, clogging his lungs, or catching on some dangerous STD, or self-imposed lung cancer. His job was one that many people envied but few would dare trade shoes with him. He killed people—bad people. And every second on the job, he knew it could be his last. Meditation served both to slow things down and improve his focus. He was so used to it now that he could go for an hour straight.

He picked up his backpack and began the descent from the steep granite rock dome. The wind whispered across the plain. He calmed his breath. Less oxygen at that altitude. The heavy gray clouds signaled they were on the verge of spitting a downpour. He smiled. He liked to run in rain. Which happened often in these eastern highlands of the country. Torrents.

He was a ghost, and everything he owned was in that backpack. Well, anything of value to his survival. He carefully climbed down, watched the village in the valley, deciding whether to go back. The thatched huts stood like tiny mushrooms from where he was. He didn't want to say goodbye. He had left unannounced too many times, and no one worried. Grandma Grace always left his room open for him. Each time he left for weeks or months, he would always find his room as neat as he had left it. He had tried to buy them a well, but Grandma Grace wanted to drink water from the local spring. Six preferred that spring water, too. Honestly, it tasted better. He walked towards the village, passed a few boys and girls playing soccer with a plastic ball tied together with strings. Barefoot. He passed by the school. Two auditoriums joined into one. Six had sponsored these and a borehole to supply the students with clean water. Some walked miles and miles to come to school. He could afford to do more, and he had wanted to do more, but he didn't want to raise eyebrows. When good things start happening, he knew people would start asking questions. And he didn't want any attention. His job depended on it. To the world, he didn't exist apart from Grandma Grace.

Six reached his room, packed a few bottles of water, and headed to the kitchen. This was the main hut at the center. Grandma Grace sat by the fire, left leg crossed, kneading the *sadza*, a concoction of cornmeal and water, over the fire. She smiled and told Draye he was just in time for supper. Draye obliged and sat on the built-in bench of mud and clay plastered with cow dung. The entire room smelt of fresh cattle dung, in a good way. And the floor was green. Six liked it. Maybe he had simply grown to appreciate everything. The floor was green, and some dung plaster still damp. He adjusted to the smoke as the carbon dioxide, monoxide, and soot filled his lungs. This was the only part he hated about staying here. He squinted through the heavy smoke and thanked Grandma Grace, who slid him a plateful of *sadza* and vegetables. This also Six liked. Locally sourced ingredients, no meat, except for Christmas and New Year holidays. She was probably his only living relative that he knew about, and that was enough.

Grandma Grace noticed Draye's backpack. She knew he was leaving—for now. He finished eating and thanked her. He handed her a few hundred-dollar bills, which she crumpled and stuck under her bra and the head cloth she was wearing. He made her promise she would get something nice for herself. She said yes, but Six knew she would spend the money on others anyway. She told him to be safe, and he exited the hut into the fresh air.

Six checked his watch. He had to trek the seven and half kilometers to the bus stop. He hoped he would find a ride. Even though he could afford to buy a car, he preferred not to. He hated standing out or drawing attention. Plus, with his job, he couldn't be in one place for long. One minute here, the next across the globe. He blended in. He found some peace in having less. He didn't have to be attached to stuff. He enjoyed the little things, like bathing in the river: He would sometimes watch as the soapy water washed down, as if exfoliating all the stains he had from killing people, bad people. Powerful people he classified as belonging to the great beyond. Well, as far as he was concerned.

The sun was descending and close to the

horizon. It would take him an hour to get to the nearest bus stop, but that was alright. It would be dark then, but that was okay too. Darkness did not scare him. He was a weapon himself. He feared only wild animals and cobras known to frequent the area. But even then, the odds of his survival were high. He slid his backpack on and trudged along.

CHAPTER
TWO

A THOUSAND KILOMETERS AWAY, Reggie Kona stared at the documents spread on the wooden floor of her bed and breakfast. She checked her phone. It was 11:50 p.m. *Late!* She finished the last drop of coffee from her mug. She had finished the entire pot of the tasteless complimentary hotel room coffee. Today she didn't care, she only wanted caffeine. Anything to keep her awake. She had promised herself to finish reading the reports today. Reports from the sea-divers, the local police, and the park rangers on duty that day, neatly piled on the carpet. Nothing pointed to a malfunction. There was nothing helpful. This was the first time someone had fallen in the Zambezi River and their remains, or pieces of them, had not been found. Bodies and the inflatable rafts both missing? No way. The bodies, she could understand, but for the float tubes to disappear as well? This was a first in the history of rafting along the Zambezi. And the missing teenagers' case particularly bothered her. Something was not lining up. She had studied files and files on the plane, but nothing.

She looked at the photo of the six kids, taken hours before their descent to the river. They looked happy. She wondered who in their right mind would go rafting in the crocodile- and hippo-infested waters. But people did. She guessed it was for that beastly feeling to play with death. She kind of envied them. But she did the same, except she took risks to keep others safe, not for thrills. Her agency always got called for vexatious matters.

She placed the photo back into the folder and replayed on her phone the helicopter search footage from one of the cold cases she had re-quested. The video was taken a few hours after the tourists and their guide had failed to report back to camp. There were crocodiles here and there, and locals fishing at positions along the river. Still nothing. *Just another accident.*

Someone knocked on her door.

"Reggie, can I come in?" the voice said.

"Yes, Clive, come in."

Clive opened the door and stood, hands on waist, his paunch hanging. He sighed. "You're still up?"

"What's up?" Reggie said, without shifting her gaze from the paper she was reading.

"They don't pay us enough for this!" Clive moaned. "I can't even buy enough groceries or send money to my wife back home."

Reggie shrugged. "You could, if you stopped drinking and gambling."

"I miss the days when I was a simple cop. I made a ton of money from bribes on roadblocks. We would make up shit just to make sure someone paid something under the table. In those days money was nothing."

"That's abuse of power."

"What do you expect when the government refuses to pay its civil servants?"

"Like I always say, you're in the wrong profession if you got into it to be rich."

Clive threw himself into the armchair. "Any luck?"

"No. Nothing yet."

"There is nothing. We are wasting our time."

"Are we?"

"Yes. We should chase big fish. Not some American kids missing. Everyone knows crocodiles ate them."

"We don't know that yet."

"Come on, it's the Zambezi River!"

"We have a week to find that out."

"And a waste of time."

Reggie remained quiet.

"So where do we start?" Clive said.

"We start where it all started."

"The Falls?"

"Yes. Meet me up there tomorrow at 6:30 a.m."

"That's early. Who wakes that early in a paradise like this unless for an early-morning safari?"

"But we are not on a safari, partner."

Clive shrugged. "Okay, I will."

"If I don't see you, I will go by myself. No drinking tonight!"

"Yes, partner. Gotta stay clean for the job."

"You'd better."

"See you tomorrow."

"Good night."

Clive closed the door and left for his room.

CHAPTER
THREE

THE JOLT SHOOK HER. She felt the small hands timidly touching her. Her svelte frame swayed from side to side. She paused, letting her eyes adjust to the darkness. Even in the dark, she could see the terrified eyes. She touched a hand. There was something. A bracelet. "Thank you," she whispered, then embraced the small girl who was resting her head on her shoulder. She shed a tear. She saw the other silhouettes. Everyone was now awake and shaken.

It had been a couple of hours since disembarking at Beira Port in Mozambique. She was seasick, but she felt for the little girls. She felt sorry. Some of them had been torn away from their families, and some had been sold freely. She wiped grime from her face, observing a thick layer of dirt on the back of her hand. The container smelled of human scent—filthy human scent. The container had been their bedroom, dining room, and toilet for the past forty-eight hours. It had been a month since they had departed the Port of Shanghai. That was the last time she had walked on the ground. They saw light only when the metal door swung open, usually at night, when the angry men threw them stale loaves of bread and water bottles. Their only meal of the day. Lin was used to the darkness. She couldn't sleep from the massive equipment all around them, continuously clinking with each bump.

From her mind mapping, she knew they had traveled northwest, but couldn't pinpoint the location. If her intel was correct, they should be near Victoria Falls by now. She had counted the handful of times the fleet of trucks had stopped at roadblocks, something common in Zimbabwe, but no one searched the contents. She knew why. You could get away with anything through bribery around here.

She had mapped the walls of the container the few times the doors opened and scraps of stale bread and water were thrown in. No cameras. She felt her muscles slightly weak. It's amazing what a few weeks of sunlight deprivation did to one's body. Even in the dim light, she could see signs of Vitamin D deficiency in the girls, which, coupled with the hopelessness, made things worse. She spent hours on push-ups and burpees in the dark, difficult in the crammed space. Her eyes had even adjusted to the blank darkness.

· · ·

SHE CONSOLED the little girl in Vietnamese. The girl's eyes were filled with fear. She clung to Lin's hand as the heavy metal lock bar unlatched with a clink. There was nothing good that came when that door opened. They waited, shielding their eyes from the blast of light to follow. Coarse voices instructed them to come out quietly, and the girls filed out of the truck. Lin knew that even if they cried, no one would hear from here. She saw one man with a gun. A bigger man stood next to the exit, assessing, either holding kids back or shoving them forward. When he got to Lin he paused, smiled, and seemed satisfied. "This one!"

Lin looked at the man. The man smirked. "Move!"

He shoved Lin to the side. She fell to the curb, where a few other elected girls sat.

When the container was emptied, the truck left. The big man looked at Lin, the disgusting grin still on his face. "You are coming with me!"

The other man with the gun shoved Lin towards the man. He seized Lin's hand. She wanted to break his nose, and looked for help at the other frightened girls. They did not move. He smelled her hair. "I'm going to have some fun with you. You smell like crap!" he said. His men laughed.

"Okay, boys. Take them to camp. We have seven days until the big day. Make sure they are spotless."

His subordinates obliged, though in displeasure at being sent back to work empty-handed.

Lin shivered, stepping back from the big

man. Her skin was all black spots from several nights in the container. She gripped the earth with her feet so that the man had to yank her forward.

"I'm going to have fun with you. Move!" the man said.

She trembled, but was somehow happy it was herself and not the kids. He led her past the main gate that enclosed the prefab settlement.

CHAPTER
FOUR

SIX PASSED a few high-school boys and girls running home. He understood some of them walked for hours to get to school and for hours to get back home. His father had often told him how he used to walk ten miles a day. It was dark. Crickets and other nocturnal creatures were chirping full blast. Frogs croaked down by the creek. An owl or two hooted as Six passed the stretch of forest into the section lined with tree plantations and macadamia trees. He passed three women carrying massive straw baskets with bananas, mangos, guavas, and avocados, leaving the bus station in haste. Six felt sorry for them. One had an infant strapped to her back. They filed to the side of the road as he approached and passed, keeping as much distance as possible. Bad things happened to women in these parts, Six had heard. Yet these women had no choice but to come to the main road to sell their produce, and leave by day's end, and likely get home and cook for the husband. Six hated that setup. He had never been married, but he wondered what made these men lazy and tyrannical. He had seen the culture: Women worked like donkeys. They woke up at dawn, started the fire, warmed up bathing water for the husband, cooked breakfast, worked in the field, prepared children for school, fetched firewood sometimes walking long distances, fetched water in big buckets from the river, cooked lunch, served the husband, ate less. Same cycle again tomorrow and every day, while husbands got wasted on alcohol. He hated every bit of it. That was the culture. A culture that suppressed women. That's why he had started an anonymous scholarship for girls at the local village primary and high schools. He knew educated women would not tolerate being treated that way any longer. They would stop depending on their husbands for money, they would be independent, they would give their children better lives.

Six noticed the women's trepidation, and he stood at a distance to make them feel safer. He was a large man. Most people would be afraid of him, especially his stature at six feet five, all muscle. He was bigger than many average men. Back home in America, someone would be calling the police on him for just walking down their street. And the police would probably tase him just for being a big black man. He asked the women what they were selling, in their native Shona language. The women hesitated. Six took out some bills and told them that he was going to the bus station. He left his hands in the open to show that he didn't have any weapons. The women relaxed. One answered that they were selling bananas.

"One dollar for ten," the woman with the baby on her back said.

"Can I get ten?" Six said.

The women looked at each other without saying a word. As if by some telepathic communication, one woman unloaded her basket and put ten large bananas in a plastic bag. She started walking towards Six. She was still unsure, but she needed the money.

"I'll take the mangos and avocados too."

The women looked surprised. They packed avocados and mangoes as well and set them down so the first woman would carry them to Six.

Six handed her a hundred-dollar bill. He withdrew two more bills for the other two women.

"We can't take that," she said, handing back the money.

"But it's a gift from me."

"Why? That's too much."

They all still looked unsure.

"Take it. Get something nice for your families."

He took the bag and stepped back.

"Have a good evening, ladies."

They all smiled, clasped their hands, and bowed a little in appreciation. Six thanked them for the food and picked up the bags.

"You're not from here, are you?" one woman said.

"Is it that obvious?"

"Well, yes. If you are going to the station at this time."

"Should I be concerned?"

"It will be hard to find transport this late."

"There should be one or two at least."

"I wouldn't take those lifts," she said.

"We have problems with *Magandanga* here. Those men who kill people for their body organs."

Six looked unflustered.

"For what?"

"Black magic! To get rich."

"Why not just work hard and smart?"

"These aren't stories. This stuff happens."

"They are here?"

"Several people have disappeared."

"Do people know who they are?"

"No. But there are rumors it's the guy who owns the grocery store a few miles down the main road."

Six nodded. He thanked the women for the warning and kept walking. His gut clenched. He had never been superstitious. He believed superstition was for lazy people, a kind of willful ignorance that left people at the mercy of circumstance—for people who dodged responsibility for their own role in being where they were in life. He wasn't afraid of whatever awaited him. In fact, he hoped they would pick him up.

CHAPTER
FIVE

THE BIG MAN'S bodyguard helped him out of the Land Cruiser—a $100,000 gift from the government. But his had been customized with a few extras added to push up the price to just shy of $400,000. That covered deflation-resistant tires and ballistic-resistant chassis and glass. Shipped to Ireland, modified, and shipped back. A drop in the bucket compared to the millions he had been stealing from the country for decades. Several other bodyguards wearing dark sunglasses surrounded the car, sweeping the area for any threats. Days earlier, several had been sent ahead to make sure things were safe. The minister, although there never had been an assassination attempt on him, took every precaution.

The rear doors of the SUV opened. Two young escorts emerged.

"Come on, ladies," the minister said, in a hoarse voice from decades of smoking cigarettes.

He coughed once and spit mucus into the nearby shrubs.

They both scrambled to his side.

He lit a cigar and took a bottle of tequila in one hand. And hugged the women, one on each side. He blew smoke into the face of the one on the left, who choked, coughed, and smiled.

"You like it, don't you?" he said.

The woman chuckled back. She was clutching a red Chanel handbag.

He led the two women towards the VIP suite. One bodyguard stood at the door and held it open.

The minister turned to the Chinese man on his right.

"Good evening, boss," the man said.

"Liu, any updates?"

"One hundred million dollars in so far. Everyone is locked in."

"That's my boy," he laughed. "We are about to make a killing! Guinea pigs doing okay?"

"Yes, boss."

"Are you feeding them well?"

"Of course, boss."

"Good. And the intruders?"

"We've contained them."

"That's what I like to hear."

The minister looked at the guard at the door.

"Joe, no disturbance tonight. I need to rest. Busy day tomorrow."

"Yes, boss."

The minister, feeling the tequila, staggered forward.

"Now, ladies. Who's ready for some fun?"

The girls blushed under the front porch light, but said nothing.

"Adios!" the minister said, waving his hand at his men lined outside.

He slammed the door shut.

CHAPTER
SIX

THE BUS STOP was at a T-junction where the gravel road merged into a narrow, paved strip. The waiting area itself was nothing more than an embankment, bare, all the grass dead from stomping, punctuated on both sides by two tall gum trees. On one side was a heap of rotting fruits and fruit peelings, overflowing from the drainage ditch; the stench was awful. On the other were piles of trash—plastic, water bottles, paper, and more. It was 7 p.m., yet the place was already dark and deserted.

Six sat on the grass ridge next to rows of tea plants. He ate two bananas and a mango and threw the peelings into the ditch. The sky was clear, filled with stars. He marveled at the clear sky, mapping the stars, trying to see if he could find the Big Dipper. Six lay down resting his head on his backpack, reminiscing about how he used to do the same when he was young, whenever his parents brought him to see Grandma

Grace. The humid afternoon had turned cooler. The weather was perfect.

He was still deep in thought when he heard footfalls on the mulch between the tea rows behind him. Slow-silk crashing—not an animal. Six reached for and unlocked his SIG pistol, on the ready, while remaining lying down. He waited. He mapped the footfalls. He waited some more. The footfalls changed course, and the sound faded away moments later. He guessed it must have been a wild animal after all. He waited for thirty minutes, then decided to walk. The closest town was only twenty miles away. He would be there before dawn. He shouldered his backpack and walked on.

The narrow road became more deserted as the night wore on. He checked his wristwatch. It was now 8 p.m., and he still had sixteen miles to go to reach the nearest town. His army combat boots crunched against the gravel. Heavy boots, which reminded him of his Marine Corps training days.

Thirty minutes later, he noticed a faint light coming through the wattle-tree plantation all around and ahead of him. He looked, but whatever had cast the light was far away, back behind the wattle trees. He saw the light before hearing the sound. The engine growl became audible. A Land Cruiser, he could tell. It became louder and the lights brightened as the car got closer. Six stood on the pavement and raised his thumb. The cruiser slowed and pulled up next to him.

It was one of those Land Cruiser 79 series known for their durability. He guessed the car had seen a couple hundred thousand miles. Probably a late 1980s model. He thanked heaven and walked to its window. There were two men in the front. The older, staunch one on the passenger side spoke.

"Where to?" the man said.

"Town."

The man looked at the driver, who nodded.

"Hop in the back."

Six saw there were other passengers already crammed in. "Can we all fit?"

"Yeah. Squeeze in. We got to help each other, right?"

"How much is it to town?"

"Don't worry about it."

"I've the money. I can pay."

"We are going that way anyway."

Six thanked them.

He squeezed into the truck bed, hunched in with three other men. He forced the rear doors shut. It was so tight that he could barely breathe or move a muscle. His knees pressed against his hunched torso. The car hissed on. In a moment, an eerie silence befell the car, often intercepted by only a creak here and there from the old car chassis when the truck ran over a pothole. Six tried easing the tension.

"You all going to town?"

"Yes!" the man next to him answered. His stench was heavy with *sope*, a local vodka, and some marijuana. *Sope* was a concoction of crushed corn, bananas, sugar, and yeast, which was boiled, fermented for a week, boiled again, and purified using makeshift fractional distillation tools to produce a killer spirit. There were rumors that some local brewers even added fertilizer to increase the buzz. Six had tried it and knew how strong it was, probably eighty percent alcohol content. He wondered how many livers this local favorite had scorched or how many people it had sent to the grave. He could see the two people in the front through the back glass. The driver cracked the window and asked where Six was going in town. Six asked to be dropped off at the post office, which was next to the main road. Six observed the other passengers, all men. They did not smile. They were all massive and lean. Possibly from manual labor on the farms. They stank of cigarette smoke and marijuana, almost choking Six. They stared at him coldly, through bloodshot eyes, sizing him up. The air was tense. Six set his backpack atop his legs, and set the bags of fruits wherever he could. He offered some, but none of the men replied. He got the message and sat quietly.

A few moments later, the car drove off the paved road. The road became bumpy. Six mapped the path in his head. They had veered eastward. The driver said they were circumventing a police roadblock just outside the town limit. The driver cursed the corrupt police, who always took money. He also said this was the shortest way, though rough. Six waited. He could feel the car going the opposite way. He waited a few more minutes.

"When are we getting there?" he said.

"Soon. A few more minutes."

Six sensed the other men tense.

The truck bumped over potholes and stopped. The driver walked to the front, checked the tires and under the car. He walked around to the passenger side and told the old guy they had a flat tire. The old man ordered everyone out. The driver dimmed the lights. The man beside Six spoke for the first time. He ordered Six to get moving. Six obliged. He knew what was coming. The man snatched Six's backpack when Six tried to pick it up. The other men got out of the car.

"Get out!" the man holding his backpack said.

From his tone, whatever this was, Six could sense it was not good. They were murderers, but Six guessed they didn't want to dirty the car seats with blood. Six studied the surroundings. The area was dark, except for the faint moonlight. They were somewhere about ten minutes southeast of the town. There were trees and long grass everywhere. No one would hear anyone who yelled for help from here. The thugs knew that. And that seemed to give them some animalistic confidence. They all acted possessed now. Ripping the soul from another human being was not that easy. That's why they had to be so high, their blood pumping. And even for seasoned murderers, the ordeal was frightening. Marijuana and booze were the only things that kept them from going insane. Six knew that. Even though his job was killing high-profile bad guys, the action of taking someone's life changed you forever. He never wanted to take any life unless pushed. Thankfully, yoga and meditation helped him, and he didn't smoke and rarely drank. Knowing that every evil soul he extinguished made the world a better place gave him some solace, even though there would always be bad guys, evil people, no matter how many he killed.

The old man ordered Six to hand over his wallet.

"You can have all my money, but let me go," Six said, leaning on the vehicle. That tactical move gave him a vantage point to see all five guys and prevent blindside attacks.

"I said, give me your wallet!"

Six complied and handed the wallet to the man on his right, making sure not to reveal the SIG pistol holstered to his side. The man fiddled with the wallet under his cellphone light. He observed Six's Zimbabwean I.D. card, obtained through his paternal grandparents. The man tossed it to the ground. Six flinched. He was getting irritated. Six was thankful he carried only the minimal required documents. Then the old guy found Six's wooden club.

"What are you? A cop?" the man said, waving the wooden club.

Six did not answer.

"What do you need this for?"

"Just a citizen who likes art."

The old guy snorted. "Thanks for the present."

The driver searched the rest of the wallet and bag.

"Five hundred dollars? Where do you work to get this kind of money around here?"

"In the city."

"I can see that. Your skin looks like you stay in the shade all the time. Where do you work?"

"Clerk."

"City boy, huh?" one man said.

"You must be a big clerk," another said.

"I guess so."

One man spat. The other men laughed. Six laughed too.

"Funny, huh? You think this is funny?" the short old man said, waving the wooden club in his right hand. He was dressed better than the others. He was probably their boss.

"Yes, this is super fun."

"We shall see. On the ground!"

"That, my friend, I will not do."

All the men unsheathed machetes. They stood sneering, grimacing, waving the weapons.

Six stood still.

"Guys, let's not do this."

"They all say that, until I rip their hearts out, drink their blood, and cut their genitals off," said the old man, exaggerating the motion with his hand.

Six sneered at this. He hated wasting time.

"I don't want to do this. You let me go, I let you live."

"You must be dreaming. Let us live? You should be crawling, begging for mercy. Or saying your last prayers."

Six looked down at the old man, then at his crew. "You mean all these big men are your bitches?" he scoffed.

The other men raged, waving their machetes and circling Six, fuming.

"You will die tonight."

"You're the guy people have been talking about. Police are looking for you all over this place. People are afraid of you here."

"I own this town," the man said.

Six noticed pride in the man's voice. The old man smelled the tip of his knife, and displayed what looked like an old Smith and Weston revolver strapped to his belt.

"Yes, you own this town," Six said. "Driving that beat-up truck. And owning a rundown grocery store with no electricity. Things are going pretty well for you."

The man foamed.

"You are wanted across this region. I also know you are a coward. You keep running, working in the shadows," Six smirked. "I can't tell which one. Either you are a pussy or you're just a wannabe. Tell me, which is which?"

"You think you are clever, huh? I will eat you alive!"

"Shoot me then?"

"I'm going to rip your heart out and eat it."

Six laughed, all the while calculating.

"Normally I let my victim's misery end fast," the old man said. "But for you I'll make an exception. I will enjoy making you suffer. You and your big mouth—"

"As you wish." Six turned as if to open the vehicle's door.

Right then, one man lurched forward. Six dodged to the side, letting the man slam his head on the door's narrow edge. He groaned, holding his forehead. Six punched him in the gut. The man flailed to the ground; his machete flew into the grass. He groaned and writhed. The boss signaled to the others. They lunged at him. Six dodged, using his jiujutsu move to deflect the blow and send one man stumbling into the other, felling them both. It was so easy, Six thought. The third man charged straight at him. Six deflected his body and elbowed the man in the back of the neck, then slammed the man's head into the side windshield with such force that both his skull and the car window cracked. And the man collapsed, unconscious. The other men were up and charged at him, waving and slashing the air. Six dodged, cracked one man's elbow, immediately disarming him. He screamed in pain and the machete sailed to the side. Six used him as a shield against the other charging man. That man screamed as his compatriot's machete slashed his trunk. The third man slashed the air and charged. Six deflected his move, using the attacker's momentum to slam the man onto the ground on his back, tranquilizing him with a blow to the carotid. He lay motionless.

He could see the fear in the boss and driver, who seemed unsure of what to do next.

"Let's kill him!" the boss shouted, brandishing a gun in one hand and machete in the other.

Six had been ready. With the butt of the machete, he hit so fast that both men fell to the ground on top of each other, motionless.

Six bound the three dead machete-wielding men together, then the other two. He then heaved all the bodies into the truck bed, making sure he snapped the boss's neck. With a sharpie from his backpack, he labeled all of them on the forehead. He wiped the blood on his hands on the grass and cursed, wiped blood off the wooden club and put it back in his bag. It was a family treasure, and Six just liked it. A gift from his grandmother. She said his great-grandfather had carved it from a sickle bush tree back in the nineteenth century when the family had made the trek from the south. He had been a great warrior. The club, which broadened from handle to head, was carved with cobras along its length. Several of the patterns were damaged, with rugged edges, evidently from hitting people. Six always wondered. Despite the damage, the wooden club was still ten times stronger than most of the Chinese ones.

He slammed the cruiser into drive and headed north. That should lead to the road.

Six wrapped his hand with a cloth from his backpack. His hand had blocked a weapon and it hurt like hell. The tooth mark on his knuckle came from knocking out a tooth of one of his former comrades. Back then, nicknamed Six, he was known as a hothead. Four tours in the Middle East. Discharged from the Marines for a misdemeanor before being recruited by a covert organization. He had broken the noses of four soldiers bullying a local farmer in the Middle East. He had always hated bullies. He had started exploring his family roots while in mandatory recovery classes.

He pondered what to do with the bodies. He

could turn them in to the police, but that would eventually blow his cover, and he also understood what happened to vigilantes. The police had tendencies to screw people who did well the job they were failing to do.

Minutes later he reached the police station off the main street. He dumped the bodies, drove past, then phoned the main police office and watched from a distance as the four police officers on duty stood flabbergasted at the bodies lying at their front door. They immediately called the regional police and told them to enforce the perimeter.

"This one is dead, but still warm!" one officer said, after checking one of the bound men.

"This one is alive."

"I wouldn't want to be him!"

"They're going to be chewed to pieces."

Moments later, several more police cars arrived with blaring sirens. Six put the cruiser in gear and sped off. The fuel tank was full, with an extra several gallons packed in the back. The driver's fake license was there. A long drive ahead.

Moments later he reached the police roadblock at the city limits. He drove slowly past the oil drums placed in the middle of the road and rolled down his window. A man in police uniform walked over. Six handed him twenty dollars. The policeman thanked him and signaled his comrade to open the barricade and let Six through. They never asked to see his license. He drove on.

CHAPTER
SEVEN

SIX ENJOYED BEING ALONE. It allowed him to think about things, issues that most people nowadays had no time for. While most people spend hours buried in smartphones and social media, Six liked it out here. Only himself, the road, and nature. It was self-therapy. He felt alive, in connection with every nerve, every muscle fiber in his body. He could just think, apart from the driving on the wrong side of the road and having to swerve occasionally from oncoming traffic at intersections.

Six's father, Sixpence Senior, joined the army as a medic after graduating from college. Easiest way to get permanent residency. His father was his hero growing up. He remembered people saying, "Thank you for your service"; thank you for this, thank you for that. Respect wherever they went. After putting himself through community college as an average football player, linebacker, Six had carried on the family legacy. The marines offered plenty of possibilities—free tuition at college, a livable wage, and he could get some okay healthcare at the local V.A. Cheap, just like his last name.

After finishing his six years in the marines with four Middle Eastern tours under his belt, Six had called it quits. Or rather, he was forcibly retired. Being home was difficult. He missed his old buddies, the rush of being in action. And things were different—work, people— everything.

One day he found a photo of himself and his grandmother, and backpacked to Africa to find her. That would give him some peace and some purpose. The name of the village was written on the back of the blurred image. Six had faint memories of visiting his grandmother when he was little. But that was two decades ago. His father had talked about her a lot. He did not know where she lived in town; eventually he found her after asking almost sixty people from the local township, with a commercial district comprised of one store. And so he had done for six years now. It was on one of these trips that they contacted him—the secret organization. A private contractor calling themselves NEPHRON. They handled several issues, ranging from corruption to kickbacks, to trafficking. He enjoyed being in new places. It was interesting: In Europe, no one cared about him. At home in America, he was often discriminated against. In Africa, he fit right in. It was an easy decision to accept the invitation.

CHAPTER
EIGHT

LIN PULLED hard while her knees pressed the back of the big man's neck, each pull digging the electrical cord farther into the man's neck, constricting his airways. The man kicked, flailed, then lay still. Dead. She let go of the cord and stumbled to the bathroom.

Lin washed her face and hands and dried herself with the cloth hanging above the sink. She looked in the mirror, stained with droplets of toothpaste and more. She looked different, could easily pass as a teenager. The layers of disguise looked natural. The miniskirt, the dyed hair tied in a double ponytail, eyelashes, bright-red lipstick, the high heels, and the fake brand-name bag. She straightened her padded bra, dumping the stuffing in a plastic bag. Everything was fake. The makeup artist and dresser had done a good job. Satisfied, she went back to the lounger and looked at the dead body on the floor, her hair clip still stuck through his Adam's apple. Streaks of blood painted the white wall. Even after death, the man was still begging for life. She kicked his outstretched hand, the hand that had tried to reach for a gun. She wiped up blood with the dead man's shirt and bagged the hairclip. "Sorry, my friend. Accidents happen. But I think you deserved this one," she whispered to herself. She stepped over the body, lit the cigar lighter, and threw it over the thin mattress and blankets. She waited a few more seconds until the blaze was high, then exited the tent. A few minutes later, the gallons of gasoline outside the tent exploded, sending a ball of red flames into the sky. Loud noises erupted as neighbors rushed to put out the blaze, to no avail. Lin walked off. She had studied her way around. Just around the corner, she boarded a taxi to the Safari Club.

LIN ARRIVED at the Safari Club around the same time as another visitor arrived. She noticed the guy across the room looking at her.

Her contact arrived a few minutes later.

"You look fabulous," the contact said.

"Thanks, Jess. They did a good job with the disguise. Do you think they will like me?"

"Of course. Which man wouldn't? You look like a snack. They will drool over you."

"I hope I come out alive."

"Oh, come on. Don't give me that look. You have done more dangerous things than this."

"I know. But it never gets easy. Our client is ruthless."

"I know. You can do this."

Lin sighed.

"And just know that we are there for you."

"Thanks, boss."

"You can get out when you feel like it. You did your job. The team is working on tracking the accounts. We can send in a team once we have solid evidence."

"No. I need to see this through. Something big is happening soon. And your bureaucracy will take days to get approval. We don't have that much time."

"It doesn't matter. You could go."

"I could, but as a victim of trafficking myself, this is now personal," she said.

"The agency can't help you with that."

"I understand."

Jess remembered the first time she saw Lin, a scrawny kid in dirty clothes, during their raid of a London high-crime neighborhood. How Lin had been saved by the agency, after jumping from foster home to foster home, until she joined the unit after high school. From the onset, Jess knew the girl was bred for this kind of work. She was one of her best assets.

"You're so stubborn. If you do this, you're on your own."

"I know that."

"Okay. Be careful."

"Always."

"I've all your things in your room." Jess handed Lin the room key card.

"Did you get my request?"

"Yes. Your new identity and credentials are

all in there. Kai, a journalist for the New York Daily."

"Great. Thank you." Lin hugged her and headed out to her suite.

CHAPTER
NINE

SIX REACHED HWANGE, a town about a hundred kilometers from Victoria Falls, late in the afternoon. The air was humid, thick with coal dust. Even though he was used to globetrotting, this trip had been hard, driving the rugged old cruiser, bribing several police guards on several roadblocks, which seemed to him to be at the entrance and exit of every city. The local police always found something wrong with your car: a broken light, cracked windscreen, chipped paint, whatever they could manufacture to make you pay bribes. He had given forty dollars away. It was not much, but it still annoyed him to give that away to crooks who misused the law they had sworn to protect. Too many potholes in the narrow, unmarked roads. On some unmarked roads, drivers had to show their turn signals to the opposing oncoming traffic to know where the middle was. He had taken a detour after a bridge recently built by a Chinese company had collapsed after a flood, which added more hours to his trip.

Six passed an enormous billboard labelled in giant letters, "Special Economic Zone," with an image of a yet-to-be-built mega-hydro power station. He had read about it in the newspaper. Pundits argued that the special economic zone was just a fancy way of saying that out here you could do business without the government breathing down your neck. It was tax-free—for at least a couple of years. And the government, seeking foreign investment, often relaxed the vetting process of foreign investors as long as they brought money in. The entire process was riddled with corruption, with foreign investors vying for opportunities at a top destination like Victoria Falls, which were often made possible through kickbacks to prominent politicians.

Six ditched the truck behind a pile of excavators rusting by the roadside just outside the city, wiping away all fingerprints. Upon project completion, these heavy machines were often left to rot. He proceeded to a dimly lit convenience store and headed inside. He was tired and didn't want to talk much. He stretched his stiffened back. The signpost indicated they were about thirty kilometers into the city. This was good. The cashier was sitting behind one of the few candles that lit the store. Six nodded at him.

"You're lucky we just got gas last night," the man said.

"Is that a big deal?"

"We haven't had petrol for over a week now.

If you came yesterday, the gas queue went all the way back to the main road for a few kilometers."

Six nodded. "That's crazy."

"Petrol is the new gold here."

"So I heard. Sorry, I don't drive much. I just squeeze in buses. It's cheap and I don't have to worry about this."

"Unless the gas station is owned by the government," the man said. "Then you get the first preference."

"Anything wrong with that?"

"Everything. I've never been a fan of the state running all businesses. It makes people lazy, always expecting handouts. Instead of supporting us hardworking businessmen, incentivizing us. That's why everything in this country is substandard."

"Never been a fan of the government myself."

Six picked up a soda from the fridge. Rugs were stuffed under the fridge to catch water from the ice melting. He ordered a to-go plate of rice and stew from the lady cooking, assisted by a boy, probably her son. He headed to the checkout.

"Four ninety-nine," the man said.

"Great," Six said. He handed him a fifty-dollar bill. "Keep the change."

"Sir, that's—"

"It's all right. You need it."

"Thank you, sir."

"One more thing," Six said. "You can keep the car."

The man hesitated, glancing towards his wife and their son. "The car?"

Six pointed towards the truck behind the pile of excavators. He handed him the keys.

"Won't the police come looking for it?"

"I doubt it. You're a hustler. I'm sure you will figure out what to do. You can earn some good money for your family."

The man smiled at the compliment. He slid the keys into his pocket.

"You know an easier way to get to the city?"

"Just in time," the cashier said. He checked his wristwatch. "The Johannesburg-Lusaka overnight bus will be here any minute now."

"Thank you."

THE DOUBLE-DECKER BUS rolled in a few minutes later, and Six hopped on. He paid ten dollars to the bus conductor, who gave Six a pink receipt. The bus was humid, filled with sleepy customers. He squeezed past and stepped over piles of suitcases, boxes, and bags. He knew most of the passengers were coming home for the holidays, as everyone seemed to immigrate to South Africa for work, and maybe return once every three or four years. He found an empty seat at the back of the bus. Perfect.

The bus rolled out moments later. Six gazed through the window at the dark smoke from the thermal power station, rising from three massive smokestacks. *The culprit,* Six thought. A fourth colliery was underway, despite the United Nations call for countries to stop generating electricity from coal by 2040. In fact, a third of all world electricity was from coal plants, despite notable contributions to climate change.

Six arrived at the Safari Club thirty minutes later. The concierge offered to carry his bag to his room, which Six declined. He noticed several people in the lobby, particularly one woman on one side. He had been an avid anime fan, which is probably why she attracted his attention. Asian for sure, dressed like one of those anime characters. Really short skirt, hanging one-button blouse knotted at the bottom, revealing a toned core, and heavy makeup and lipstick. Six guessed she was Japanese from the miniskirt, shoulder-length hime haircut, and knotted blouse. She looked like a schoolgirl. Six noticed she was looking at him, too. He grabbed the keys and headed out to his cabin suite.

Six was exhausted. The cabin was beautifully designed and furnished, with floor-to-ceiling windows that allowed the view of the sprawling wildlife and a glimpse of the mist from the Falls. Everything oozed elegance. Everything was top-notch, carefully crafted, from the floor rugs on the main entrance, African quilts, mosquito nets, the leopard and zebra skins adorning the wall. But Six only wanted a bed, a shower, and a running trail.

The concierge brought in champagne and orange juice. Six drank both.

"Here you go, Mr. George," the man said.

The text from his command had used James George as his alias.

"Thanks."

"My pleasure, sir. Dinner is at seven."

"Could I get a map of the complex?" Six said. "Just to make sure I find my way around."

"It's not that complicated. But I will bring you one right away, sir."

The man retrieved the brochure from the cart and handed to Six, who thanked him and closed the door.

Six marveled at the room. Every detail in the room exuded an African charm—the mahogany furniture, giraffe skin stretching above the headboard, a stuffed elephant foot used as a stool, a tusk above the TV, straw window blinders, two leather drums next to the window, and the giraffe-designed bed covers. He guessed this was the giraffe room. Oh, and the mosquito net. The mosquito net! That was an essential in these malaria-infested parts and he had heard tales of people going insane from cerebral malaria.

An alert tone buzzed from his phone. He unlocked it and downloaded the encrypted file. Six browsed through. He hated vague missions. But they also energized him. Probably the only thing that kept him in this job. Six's mind wandered to the fateful day when his life had changed, in the marines. He forcefully brought his attention back to the present moment.

Six scanned through the file about the target. As much as he hated vague missions, that's where the thrill was. This was one. The report said an inside source had alerted the agency that the target would be at the lodge today or the next day. They had intercepted some info on something big about to happen. Nothing more, nothing less.

The high-ranking government official would be in his seventies now—the African criterion to be in power. The bastard had done atrocious things. Further digging had revealed the guy might be the same guy the FBI had been hunting for decades for atrocities in Mozambique, killing thousands of local villagers in the '80s and '90s. A girl had filed a lawsuit claiming the minister had drugged and raped her. Six's team had intercepted the confidential DNA test results by mistake and connected to matches found in other previous victims. That's what they did. This was their guy. Except now he could commit his atrocities in broad daylight. Men would bark for him if he said so. Loyal. The guy was still doing his old ways. Guess old habits never leave. The more Six read the file, the more his blood boiled. He slammed the phone on the table. He wanted to choke the life out of him, then reminded himself this was just a job.

Six browsed through the local newspaper with nothing major or interesting apart from the upcoming tigerfish-catching competition. Six even entertained the idea of participating. The front-page headline story described how immigration authorities had confiscated and burned twenty thousand pounds of ivory at the Beira Port. Six wondered if this was all connected.

REGGIE REMOVED the strap around her waist. Her heart had slowed down from the 150 beats per minute reached at the rapids at the bottom of the Victoria Falls bridge. Her dopamine was still high. She gave a victory shout, and high-fived several people waiting in line to bungee jump. The jump had been epic. Reggie liked the adrenaline rush. This was her drug. Her medicine against the pain. She lived for risky and dangerous stuff like this. She had to. She was used to it now. *Fuck pain!* She sat next to the rails and did some deep breathing. Her fitness tracker showed her heartbeat had slowed to 130 beats per minute. Sixty seconds later, it showed 56 beats per minute. Clive, her partner, was waiting by the rails farther away from the gorge, with a multitude of other revelers, away from the waterfall showers.

"How did I do?"

"Great. I thought you did great!" Clive said,

handing her a towel from her bag. "Still don't know how you people do it."

She smiled. "It's fun. You should try it some time."

Clive watched Reggie dry water dripping from her natural curls.

"I'm afraid of heights, and there's no way in hell I will voluntarily leap from the top of a bridge, one hundred and eleven meters down, into a crocodile-infested river!"

"I get your point."

Reggie used the towel to dry herself and wrapped herself in it. They walked towards the hotel.

"Anything yet?" Reggie said.

"No. It's only been twenty minutes since we talked, remember?"

"I thought the bungee jumping queue was longer than that."

"It wasn't."

"I'm going to take a quick shower. Meet you at the station."

"When?"

"Let's say at noon."

Clive frowned. "That's in forty minutes."

"Plenty of time."

REGINA KONA LIKED to work hard. Even as the lead detective for the Anti-Corruption Taskforce, she often logged eighteen-hour days. Her branch fought corruption and had brought five ministers and the Reserve Bank

Governor to justice for corruption and kick-backs. She liked to get things done. No, it wasn't hard work imposed on her. It was a kind of self-reliance that had molded her from childhood. She competed with herself. She had always done so. Growing up as the oldest of seven, taking on the parent role after her parents separated when she was ten, ploughing the field in the morning, walking five miles to school, she would come home, fetch firewood and water, cook for every-one, and still have time to read under the smoky paraffin lamp or by firelight.

In retrospect, she sometimes thanked God for a challenging childhood. Those are the moments that had shaped her. She was relentless. After she signed up to do something, she had to do it and finish—no matter what. She would stay up all night trying to solve an issue. Whatever it took. She believed in herself. Growing up in the rural areas had shaped her that way. In a patriar-chal society, the life of a girl was mapped out for her from birth: cook, fetch firewood, clean dishes, fetch water and carry it for miles, wash clothes, and get married, and have children. More children. The bar for girls was low, de-signed so they depended on a husband, who, for the most part, was abusive, given that most of them had to pay two cows to get the girl. If par-ents had two children, a boy and girl, the boy would most likely go to school while the girl helped with household chores. Fortunately, her parents separated when she was ten and her mom abandoned the children for another man.

She remembered those days like it was yesterday. She remembered scrambling for food, sleeping in the bush. Overnight she had turned breadwinner for her siblings. Her dad, bitter, violent, often beat her senselessly and the other siblings for trivial issues. She matured. She endured the five miles to school like a boss, on an empty stomach. All four years of secondary school. She made up her mind that her only way out of this situation was to get an education. The books served as an escape. She got a scholarship to a college in the U.S. She came back after four years to join the Central Investigation Department (CID), an anti-corruption taskforce created by the current president of Zimbabwe.

Because she was attractive, most of the guys in the training bootcamp crushed on her, but they all realized she was a force to reckon with. The brutal training was composed of marathons and surviving on small portions of bread for days. Graduating on top of her class, she climbed the ranks to become one of the best investigators in the agency, promoted to lead detective in the field. Something that most male officers could only hope to do.

Clive had been one of those jerks, a star rugby athlete from a prestigious high school, son of prominent ruling political party leaders. He was a bully and thought everything else in life should be handed to him. He jumped onto her one day during basic training, and she broke his nose. That was the end of it. Unlike Clive, Reggie had worked her ass off to get whatever she had and more. She knew that to beat the odds she had to work twice as hard. Nothing was handed to her. As a woman, from an unknown family with no connections, she had to. Nepotism was alive and well.

CHAPTER
ELEVEN

SIX WOKE up two hours later. He yawned and felt refreshed. The fresh linen felt good. He checked his phone. He noticed the mosquito net hanging to the side.

It was 6:15 p.m. Enough time to shower and freshen up for dinner at the clubhouse. He walked to the window. He watched warthogs and impalas grazing on the lodge grounds, unde-terred by humans.

The local handcrafted jasmine soap smelled fantastic. He chose a bright Hawaiian shirt, which suited the hot muggy Zambezi Valley weather. He smiled at the expensive decor in his clubroom, imagining how much it cost. A lot. Most of the people you would see here were rich Americans, Europeans, or recent retirees. Six had thought of staying here before, but he saw no use. He enjoyed the simple life. Only a few people could afford to stay here, but he wasn't paying for any of this, so why not? Although some would call his job dirty, it came with freedoms and luxuries that most people only dreamt of. His job allowed him to travel across the globe —for free. And he relished every moment, because in his line of work, any day could be his last.

Six opened his email and checked the file. He browsed through the details and studied his target's profile, the man's face, then and now. Six could see similarities in the man's features in the two photos, despite the two photos being many decades apart. *Money could buy you anything,* Six thought. Name change, identity, family, citizenship, and an appointment by the president as the minister of infrastructure development. He memorized the face and walked out.

On the way to the clubhouse café, he met several other tourists, some with West African t-shirts, wearing business-casual slacks, sandals, slippers. Several women wore *charis,* long, colorful, ornamented cloths wrapped around their waists. They would go home and say they had an African t-shirt, disregarding Africa as a continent of more than fifty countries, each with a distinct clothing style.

The large open area also presented the same African aesthetic: a thatched roof with exposed beams, pine smoke, candles lit above the crystal chandelier, with several fire pits around the area, where game was being slow-roasted. Six sat at the table closest to the edge, where he could see everyone coming in, and it gave him an excellent view of the clubhouses.

The front table held several casseroles and

dishes with mounds of food. With servers waiting. Wild meat, mopane worms, and more.

He watched, bemused, as a local group performed a traditional dance. The six men and six women playing drums, tambourines, and gourds with seeds, were all dressed in animal leather costumes. They sang and danced with grace and vigor, encouraging tourists to join in. He marveled at how the men stomped the pavement barefooted with such force. One woman hooked Six onto the dancing stage. Shocked, Six danced along. It felt good to relax.

At 7 p.m. the dinner bell rang, signaling the start of the multi-course feast. Six lined up for food at the serving buffet. He loaded his plate with slow-roasted wild boar, mopane worms, a mix of seasonal vegetables, and yam. Six's mouth watered. He would come back for seconds. He retreated to his small table. Moments later, four more strangers joined the table. A mom, a dad, a son, and a daughter. The children were high-school age. He learned the Bileses were from New Jersey. Six told them he was from St. Louis. They connected on the topic of baseball, basketball, hockey, everything sports. Six ordered them red wine, which the server brought immediately.

"This is my daughter Jadith and my son Jadin."

"I'm James. Nice to meet you guys."

"Athlete?" Mr. Biles said, assessing Six's physique.

"I played ball in college."

"I can tell," he said. "You're a freaking washboard."

Everyone laughed. "Blame my mom for that!" Six said.

"An athlete as well?"

"She was. A high-school champion in track and field before she bore me."

"Did you try pro?"

"No."

"Army?"

"Marines. Six years," Six said. "Joined right after college."

"Thanks for your service."

Six nodded.

The father continued, "My son plays ball. He'll be applying to Division One schools this fall."

"That's great, man," Six said. "What position?"

"Tight end."

"Nice. I bet you are a good player. You've the body and size."

The son laughed, relishing the attention.

"I hope I'll get some offers," he said.

"You will," Six said. "Keep working on your craft. Compounding. That's how you get better. If you're that good, they can't ignore you."

The boy nodded.

Six waved to the server for more wine and took a drink. He smiled at the daughter.

"What about you?" Six said.

"I want to be a doctor."

"Doctor? That's neat. What kind of doctor?"

"Ophthalmologist, probably. I hope to be a

doctor without borders, where I can travel to developing countries and help people."

"That's a good cause. I know you will do it."

The young girl smiled.

They talked about sports, climate change, some politics, the beautiful country, and many other things.

While Six chatted, he observed his target at the fifth table, where two Chinese men, three Zimbabwean men, and two Caucasian men sat dining. He recognized the minister of foreign affairs and the mayor from the hotel flyer. They all wore suits. Six guessed it must be an important meeting. They spoke with occasional laughs. He could not hear what they were saying, but could observe some intense and light moments in their facial expressions. He recognized the older black guy, Matsanga, as the minister of infrastructure development. His paunch. Six wondered how much kickback money had contributed to the man's obesity. Members of his security detail stood alert in the shadows of the clubhouse at the doors and windows. Six studied them, making sure they wouldn't notice him. His target didn't seem all that impressive. The man didn't fit the weight of his reputation. Around five feet five inches tall, overweight around the waist. Gray hair combed over his head, with bloodshot eyes, smoking a gold-banded cigar. Six forwarded the images he had taken with the camera hidden on his cap to his handler.

Moments later, a woman in a chic dress approached that table, clasping her purse. She had a local peacock-printed cloth strapped on her left shoulder. Two bodyguards stepped in to block her way. She showed them her I.D. and said something to them. One guard approached the minister of infrastructure development and whispered in his ear.

The minister signaled the guard to back off and beckoned the woman to the table.

"What's your name, young lady?"

"Kai," she said.

"Welcome, Ms. Kai." He pointed to an open seat next to himself, trying to touch her. She swatted his hand.

"Nice to meet you, Minister," she said. "Thank you for agreeing to meet with me."

"My pleasure. I look forward to our time together."

The waiter brought some wine, and Lin, seated next to her target, ordered a plate of food.

"I'm impressed, Ms. Kai. No one has ever swatted my hand like that without severe consequences."

"So does that mean you're not angry?"

He grabbed her hand forcefully. "I am. But I'm more impressed than mad. I think you and I will get along just fine. Gentlemen, since we are done with discussions, do you mind if Ms. Kai joins us?"

The woman flirted with the minister, brushing her fingers on the minister's shoulders. In response, the minister held the woman's hand. Six doubted the woman enjoyed it, but she played along, twirling strands of her hair. She swatted his hand off. The minister's face flushed a bit, then he laughed and clapped his hands. Six sipped his wine, monitoring the table without drawing attention from the guards wearing shades.

The woman's face looked familiar. Six feared what would happen to a woman among these cronies, even though he knew nothing about them, except that the Chinese were contractors. He felt something was not right. He hated bullies, especially those who took advantage of the helpless.

"So, Ms. Kai, tell me what you do again?" the minister said.

"I am a journalist," she said.

Lin watched the minister blush.

The minister knew, with so much controversy surrounding the hydro-power project, some good press would be nice. He meant to use this opportunity well.

Lin had studied the man for a few months, every move. She knew him well. Probably more than he knew himself. She also understood that a man like the minister, though displaying a tough alpha exterior, was often an insecure boy always seeking validation of his importance from worshippers. That's why he surrounded himself with "Yes, boss" followers, often traveling with an entourage of bodyguards. Lin was determined to slather praise on the man. As much as she wanted to choke the life out of him, inflating his ego was the only way to get answers and bring the operation down.

"Sir, I'm a big fan of yours. I'm here for the opening of the orphanage."

"How did you know about that?"

"It's been on the news. When I saw you here, I knew it had to do with that."

The minister smiled. "Two days from now."

"I understand the local press has not been lenient with you. I wanted to spend time with the man at the source and see if I can cast you in a better light."

"Who do you work for?"

"The New York Daily."

"Ah, New York. Go on."

"Sir, I think you're doing great work for your country. And the world needs to know that."

Lin knew men like him were paranoid. His life involved killing people and being always on the watch for assassins. Enemies were everywhere. He did not trust anyone. He was often surrounded by people who wanted to take something from him.

He glared at her, smoke from his cigar wafting. Lin stared back at the man's bloodshot eyes. He seemed to be impressed.

"Young lady, tell me about your work. Gents, where are your manners? Get the lady a drink."

Right then, a dancer pulled Lin to the stage. She jumped up and joined them.

"We've all night," she said, under the music.

Six watched the Minister observing her every move as she swayed freely with the drums. She then went back to her seat and guzzled a glass of wine. Moments later, the minister and the woman left the dining room, hand in hand, while guards surrounded them. The mayor and other big shots followed soon after.

Six waited a few minutes until a young server came to clear the table and offered Six his choice from a box of cigars.

"Are these Cubans?" Six said, picking one of the gold-banded cigars.

"I think they are MonteCristo."

"Cool."

Six pocketed one. *This gives me an idea,* he thought.

Six got up and followed the minister's group a few yards behind, with other visitors. He was surprised to see their club room was next to his. When guards glared at him he greeted them in gibberish, pretending to be drunk. The guards shoved him sidewise.

In his own room, Six quickly assembled the eavesdropping device from his backpack. Work had just begun. He would crush them if anything happened to the woman, if he heard any screams of pain. Six listened as the two people in the club room kept talking until late. She asked his opinion about all kinds of things: world affairs, the green revolution, climate change, and more. The minister talked about all his vague plans to change the world. Even though Six knew this was none of his business, he hated bullies. He had dedicated his life to stopping bullies; bullies who deprived millions of people of their birthright and resources. He just had to do it. He listened. Nothing.

CHAPTER
TWELVE

AT MIDNIGHT LIN looked at the fat man near her on the recliner, his bloated body like a sack of potatoes, arms wide open. Next to it was the empty booze glass to which she had added the tranquilizing concoction, just a little, to make the man fall into a deep sleep for eight hours. But still, he would awaken. He would remember whatever she wanted him to remember, the way she had acted it out. And he would probably ask for her to come back again. A gun was resting on the sofa table. If it was up to her, she would put a bullet through his big belly. He looked gross. Her body shivered. She quietly slid from the couch, put on her shoes, and walked out, handbag in hand.

The ashtray on the mahogany coffee table was overflowing with cigar stubs. The guy was seventy if not older, still smoking. She felt sorry for the man's lungs—how anyone could smoke that much. She shivered at the thought of how much secondhand smoke she had inhaled. She had read somewhere that the cancer-causing chemicals in tobacco were the same, whether you popped one yourself or sat next to someone smoking. She hoped it took many multiple exposures to get cancer. If all went according to plan, her mission would be done in a few days, anyway.

The guard at the front door stopped her and checked her handbag. The other one rushed into the room and checked on the minister. He saw his chest moving up and down. He didn't bother waking him, knowing how the minister never wanted to be bothered from sleep, despite his sometimes-frightening nightmares.

"Why leave so early?"

"I don't want to be seen leaving this place. I don't think your boss would want that."

The guard considered the point and seemed to agree.

"Boss is okay. You can let her go," the other guard said.

Lin gave the other man a condescending smirk and shook herself free. She tiptoed into the dark, careful not to step on animal dung, or worse, snakes. They knew where she stayed in the Safari Club, and she knew they had likely already gone there to ravage the place. Someone was maybe following her, for all she knew. But they would find nothing. Lin was a pro. To them, she was a powerless young woman. Far from the truth. She retrieved the phone that was hidden in her bra. She opened the encrypted folder. She hoped she had some of the information she needed. Most of it was in there—fingerprints, voiceprints, laptop files, few offshore account numbers, contacts, emails, browsing history—everything, all of it retrieved when her phone was resting on top of the minister's briefcase.

THIRTEEN

HE FELT the mist brushing through his skin, dampening his tank top, the morning dew on the grass soaking his running sneakers. The horizon was crimson, welcoming a beautiful dawn. He jogged past a herd of impalas grazing adjacent to the lodge. They seemed unbothered by him and kept on grazing. He reset his exercise pace tracker and jogged. The morning was cooler, the only time temperatures dropped in these parts of the country during the summer. He passed a few local vendors with big straw baskets of fresh vegetables and fruits, heading to the market on foot. He wondered how long these people walked to be here at this hour. See, that was the conundrum Six had always faced—in the overfed western world, people walked as a form of exercise, but back here people walked to survive, to get food. Other than that, the road was quiet. He passed a few safari trucks loaded with tourists on early-morning tours, with binoculars, all clad in khakis and verandah hats. That didn't interest him. He had other things in mind.

The trail wound down into the main road towards the Victoria Falls bridge. Six picked up his pace. He was aiming for eight miles per hour. His heart was still relaxed enough that he could talk comfortably if he wanted to. Four more miles to go to reach his target. The bridge was deserted except for a few shuttle buses crossing from Zambia to Zimbabwe. Six slowed down, absorbing the roars of the mighty Victoria Falls, with all the showers from the falls drenching his tank top. A stone's throw and he would be in Zambia, with the Victoria Falls Bridge over the deep gorge of the Zambezi River, which bordered the two countries. He kept on, and a few minutes later he was on the other side. The Cape Town to Dar-es-Salaam overnight passenger diesel train chimed over the Victoria Falls Bridge, leaving a cloud of smoke.

He passed the David Livingstone statue and exited the main road and took a trail that allowed for better viewing of the falls from the Zambian side, which came with more drenching guaranteed. Tourists who walked here wore raincoats if they wanted to stay dry. A sign overlooking the falls celebrated the size of the falls, and what they called the Devil's Pool. At 1,708 meters wide and 108 meters tall, the falls was among the largest waterfall in the world, rivaling Niagara Falls and Iguazu Falls, and carried the world's largest sheet of water.

Six retrieved his small pair of binoculars and checked. It was foggy everywhere, with the forbidding roar of water plummeting down. No wonder the locals had called it "the smoke that thunders." When he was about to leave, he saw something. A group of workers were ascending from the center of the falls, being pulled by a pulley on the other side of the massive waterfall. Six watched the group in wonder as the massive sheets of water pummeled them. Moments later, he understood what the group was doing. Four drones emerged from the falling water with blue lights blinking. He concluded they were surveying the area.

Six waited as the four drones descended into formation, carrying cargo, and disappeared behind the sheet of water. He waited some more. Several moments later, he heard a sound that felt like an explosion. A former marine, he had a special sense for sounds like these. He checked for smoke, a difficult task in the fog. But he noticed smoke billowing, its darkish soot. Diffusing with the mist. Strange. Was this even legal, considering Victoria Falls was protected as a UNESCO World Heritage Site? The drones emerged back out and the same sequence happened again. Well, maybe that's how the work was done.

Six continued his run and decided to go down parallel to the Zambezi River to look for debris. What he was doing was illegal and dangerous. The area was prohibited unless with a tour guide. In addition to the dangerous rapids, there were crocodiles known to eat humans. Hippos and other wild animals, including venomous snakes, called this park their home. He scrambled down the hillside onto a pebbled riverbank. The water here was crisp, clear. He squatted down and scooped the water with his hands. There was some ash, traces of it. He collected samples in his drinking-water bottle, keeping an eye out for crocodiles or hippos. He had an inkling, even though this did not concern him.

"Too early for a stroll, don't you think? And too dangerous!" a voice said from behind.

Six's heart sank for a bit. He had heard no one approaching under the loud waterfall. Bad move on his part. But then, the voice was neither aggressive nor condescending. He turned around to notice a woman standing a few yards below where he was. She was wearing a dark raincoat. She looked at him, not in a dangerous way. Six wiped off water droplets from his forehead.

"Hello," Six said, maintaining his nerves. "Now I know why they call it Mosi-oa-Tunya."

"Yeah, it's like walking in a torrent, 365 days a year," she said.

"I know."

"Why is an American hiking here this early alone?" she said, without shifting her gaze.

"Just wanted some fresh air," Six said. "I would ask the same of you," he said.

"I'm working."

"Working? Are you with those guys?"

"What guys?"

"The ones with the drones."

"They are part of the Chinese construction company. Probably surveying the area."

"I figured," Six said. He remembered

reading in the newspaper that the Chinese had won the contract to build a mega-hydroelectric power project after Victoria Falls had been designated a Special Economic Zone.

The woman flashed a badge strapped to her hip.

"Detective?" Six said.

She nodded. "I'm with the CID."

"Don't they have rangers to patrol the park?"

"They do. But there are sometimes issues that can only be handled by detectives."

"Am I in a crime scene?"

"Technically, yes."

"I wonder what that might be?"

"None of your business," she said.

"You're right. I better get going."

"What were you doing here?"

"Just taking a morning stroll. Can't stay in bed when you are in a place like this."

"Really?" the woman said, assessing Six up and down. She noticed his chiseled physique.

Six stepped closer to her with his hand stretched out.

"I am Six, by the way!"

She shook his hand firmly. "Reggie! Just Six?"

"Draye Sixpence. But all my friends call me Six."

"I see. American?"

"Yes."

"I knew it," she said.

"Why? Is that obvious?"

"Yeah. You guys like to play with fire."

"How so?"

"Haven't you heard a group has gone missing?"

"No."

"Americans, I don't know what it is about doing risky things!" she said in her native Shona language.

"I can hear you, you know," Six said in Shona.

Reggie looked at him, surprised.

"You speak Shona?"

"Yes," he said in Ndebele, another local language.

"What are you? Secret Service?"

"No. Just a regular guy with a curious mind."

She eyed him skeptically. "Yeah, right."

"My dad was Zimbabwean. Mom American."

"Sixpence? That's an interesting name. American?"

"Believe it or not, it's a Zimbabwean surname!"

"No way!"

"Dad's last name. Don't know how he got it."

"Did he change it in the US?"

"No, it goes way back to my great-grandfather."

"How so?"

"Don't ask me. My great-grandfather probably owed someone sixpence back in the day."

"I bet. Could be what they paid him for his work, cattle and land, and bondage for several generations."

"Or one of those names slapped onto him by British colonizers."

"That makes more sense."

"I asked, what are you doing? You're not supposed to drink the river water."

"Oh that? Not for drinking."

"What for?

"Tests."

"Why?"

"Seemed like those guys were blasting the rocks around the falls. I just want to know what they are using."

"You work for an environmental agency?"

"I'm a naturally curious person."

"How do you know they were blasting the rocks?"

"I saw the massive drones carrying cargo, and moments later, I think I heard an explosion."

"You sure? It's hard to hear anything else around here other than the water."

"I know I heard something."

"I'd imagine it's part of the construction process."

"Isn't that prohibited?"

"That's why the project has been stymied by discussion from the UNESCO heritage site protection agency and environmental agencies for decades. So," Reggie said, "what are you really? Special forces?"

"A digital nomad," Six said. "The world is connected now, and I thought I'd make a killing enjoying food and travel. And I'm here. What could beat this?"

She laughed. "If I was naïve, I'd believe that. I've done this work for far too long."

Six threw up his hands in surrender. "What gave me away?"

"Your physique is not of someone who lives to travel and eat. You're some hired investigator, not a digital nomad."

Six laughed. "Your English is great."

"I studied in the US."

"College?"

"Yes. Pre-medicine."

"You're a doctor?"

"American colleges take your fees as an undergraduate pre-med student, but only a handful of medical schools even consider taking one or two international students. What is your story?"

"I joined the marines right after college to get citizenship, which I did after six years."

"You could've just married a citizen."

Six raised his hands in a surrender gesture. "Do I look like someone who does that? That was supposed to be a joke."

"I know. Things are changing," Reggie said.

"I hope so."

"They are changing for this hydro project," Reggie said, pointing to the cranes and pulleys lining up below the falls. "Someone is getting really rich."

"Why hire foreign contractors to do the work, instead of employing locals? Zimbabwe is one of the most educated countries."

"It's a backward mindset. The West is better."

"Tell me about the missing Americans."

"It's an active investigation, and I don't have clearance to discuss that."

"Fair point," he said. "But from what you said, sounds like the news is public knowledge."

"It is," she said. "Here is what we know. A group of teenagers supposedly went water rafting on a birthday celebration along the Zambezi."

"Why would someone do that?"

"People do that all the time. They disappeared."

"Is that common?"

"Tourists usually have trackers and professional guides. They are thought to have been eaten by crocodiles."

"You suspect some ill activity."

"One of the teenagers is a son of a prominent American businessman. One of the major investors in the area."

"What's the game plan? Search all of Zambezi River?"

Reggie thought Six had asked too many questions.

"Go back to where you came. This area is prohibited."

"Okay. Nice to meet you."

CHAPTER
FOURTEEN

ABOUT AN HOUR LATER, the entire riverbank was packed with traffic. The search party included park rangers, local police, fire brigades, three ambulances, construction workers, and divers. Several rafts and a helicopter with darted rifles combed through the river for any signs of the missing kids. Other rafters sifted the river with hydrophone devices, tranquilizer guns, and nets. A makeshift barricade was installed upstream to reduce the river flow, allowing the search party to search upstream. Multiple stations were set up along the river, each with its own search party.

Reggie walked along the river marveling at the beehive of activity, passing by four massive, tranquilized crocodiles, one slowly being craned onto an oversized twenty-six-wheeler before being scanned by a white luminescent light. The tranquilized massive reptiles dangled on the ropes and hooks. From a distance, Six watched trucks snail up the embankment to the main road. The crocodiles were bound by chains. Never mind that they were endangered. Six wondered how many of the local people had been devoured by these local monsters.

Reggie approached the leader of the search team, who expressed despair because they had found nothing yet. But he promised to keep looking.

Reggie's partner arrived soon after.

"You're three hours late," Reggie said.

"I slept in."

"Told you, no drinking on the job."

Clive ignored her.

"Did you at least schedule our meeting with the park rangers?"

"Just finished talking to them. It's today at three."

"Awesome."

"Who was that foreigner you were talking to?"

"That foreigner," said Reggie, "has contributed to this case more than you."

"You think so?"

"Go look into him and why he took samples at a crime scene."

"I already did. You were telling our business to a professional operative, American ex-military. He killed five men the other night, a thousand kilometers from here."

"You have no way—"

"Then he gave wads of money to a storekeeper. Sometimes," said Clive, "it pays to drink with the right people! And I saw you hand him your card. You'd better be the first to call him and make him our friend."

Reggie had indeed handed Six her card, with two phone numbers and the station's address. She had told Six, "Call me anytime."

Six had studied the card. He said, "Regina T. Kona. What's the T for?"

"Thandiwe."

"That's a cool name."

"Named after my grandmother."

"What does it mean?"

"Beloved. My dad said I was the glue of the family, like my grandmother was."

"Only child?"

"I have two brothers."

"Still, you must have been loved, being the only girl."

"I'd say my grandmother was more like a slave. The name means 'beloved.' But her environment was far from it. She fetched water for miles, worked in the field, bore children, cooked for the whole family, washed laundry by hand, and fetched firewood."

"She sounds like a superwoman to me."

"She was, and she never complained."

"I'm sure she didn't know any better."

"Being a girl in her time was tough. But that's how things were back then."

Six had handed his own card to Reggie.

"Here's mine," he had said. "Wait. You don't want my card?"

Reggie had instantly memorized his number. "I gotta get to work," Reggie had said.

CHAPTER
FIFTEEN

LIN GOT off the minibus at the local shopping center. According to her calculations, it would take her about thirty minutes to walk to the mayor's mansion, most of the way through dark alleys with no streetlights. She noticed that three men got off the minibus at the same stop. She could see them following her. It was clear. *Amateurs*, she thought. She passed vagabonds loitering in the streets, most of them catcalling her. That was common, because in a highly educated society with no jobs, most young people ended up on the streets, as vendors, selling drugs, or in prison. She kept on walking.

"What's up, girl? Why are you ignoring us?" one of the men said.

Lin paused, looked at the man. He seemed to enjoy the intimidation and the cheering he was now getting from his street peers. Lin pretended she did not understand.

"Where are you going by yourself, Shortie?"

She observed the men. She understood that

hurting people always hurt other people. It somehow validated the misery they were in, channeled off their anger and uselessness and malice, hurting others. Often the innocent. She also knew most of these young men were walking time bombs, seething with pressures of missed dreams and goals, and no hope for any but a bleak future. No hope at all. Their own crime was being born in a country that wore a banner for socialism while feeding the political elite and those on top. She had no use hurting any of them unless she had to. Lin continued into the alley.

By now, the three men from the minibus had picked up pace and caught up to her. The biggest guy jumped in front and grabbed her hand. He showed the tip of the knife he held in his other hand.

Lin kept her other hand in her pocket.

"Hand over your wallet, bitch."

Lin threw a roll of twenty-dollar bills on the ground. She had been careful to leave all her valuables at the hotel.

"That's all I have."

The lead man snorted. "Lose the bag as well!"

Lin obliged. She undid the backpack and sat it on the ground.

"Am I free to go now?"

"No, bitch! You'll go when I say so," the man said.

"Let me go, and I'll leave you alone," she said.

"Oh. The bitch is making demands now."

The man laughed. The others joined in, now circling her. She waited. She shook the man's hand from her arm. The man seemed surprised by her strength, but pressed on.

"*Zhingzhong*! You come here and take our jobs. You'll pay!"

Lin had heard that word before: a word often used in southern Africa to describe goods made in China, known for their short lifespan and limited durability.

"I am a tourist, and I have taken no one's job."

"I don't care! Lose the Apple Watch as well!" the man said.

"No, this I'm not."

"Bitch, you don't have a choice," the smallest man said, waving his knife.

"You'll do as we say if you want to live," the first man said. Then he laughed. "You think we are playing. When we are done with you, you will know."

Lin had been observing that the alley was deserted. She didn't want her face on any phones, in an area where anyone could record. While the thugs saw this as an advantage, this was also what Lin preferred. She didn't want any bystanders complicating the issue.

Lin turned around and backed towards the fence such that she had all three of them in view. The first man hesitated. The two other men blocked the way. "That's enough, bitch."

She stared at the leader and took two steps. "Call me that one more time."

"Or what? Bitch—"

Before he could finish, Lin's foot collided with the man's open mouth, sending several teeth flying into the air. The man groaned in pain and crumbled to the ground, writhing. Lin rebalanced herself, standing between her items and the two other men. Their eyes shifted from Lin, to their comrade, to the money on the ground.

"Last chance. Take a bill, get yourselves some dinner and leave me alone."

Right then, one man lunged at her. Lin jumped to the side, sending the man into the fence with his momentum. He winced in pain. She sucker-punched him in the gut. The man coughed and squirmed.

The other now circled, tensed, waving his knife in wide arcs.

Lin waited.

He lunged. And Lin used his momentum to destabilize him before giving the man an upper jab. He stumbled to the ground, spitting blood.

"Kill this bitch!" the leader shouted. The rest of the crew now lunged haphazardly. One waved a knife in arcs and launched towards Lin. She dodged and kneed the guy while dislodging his grip on the knife. The man groaned and planted into the fence headfirst.

Lin checked her wristwatch. She had wasted three minutes. She didn't have time for this. She launched with a flying kick toward the guy on the left, who was still shocked at what had just happened. He tumbled onto the pavement screaming, then bolted. The other followed suit. The commotion had attracted a few spectators from among the street vendors. Lin kicked the big man still on the ground, picked up her roll of twenty-dollar bills and her backpack. She sprinted off into the dark.

"Fools! Should've just grabbed the money!" the spectators shouted.

CHAPTER
SIXTEEN

SIX TIPTOED, carefully following his mapped route. He walked, listening for any sounds. He had decided to use the backyard. He squatted, checked, darted through thick brush. Owls hooted and hyenas laughed. Out here, he worried more about being bitten by a snake than about being found by the minister's security detail. He continued, his eyes scanning side to side, up and down, always a few yards ahead. This was a perfect night. The moon would not be up for another hour, allowing Six to complete his mission with plenty of time left if everything went according to plan. His skintight suit camouflaged well with the dark. His SIG pistol was snugged across his chest, just in case. He wasn't planning on killing anyone and he hoped he would not need to, but he also knew he would if the time came. He would not hesitate. These were evil men, and evil men deserved to be eliminated when the chance presented itself, especially when they were caught off guard. Not that they were ever off guard. They were paranoid about safety.

Six put on the small night goggles. He counted five guards posted at the rear entrance. One advantage of the Club cottages was that there were no sensors. The cottages were designed to blend in with the wild. But he wanted to be careful. A man like the minister would go to extra lengths to be secure, knowing that he was one person away from dying at any moment at the hands of his many enemies or envious rivals. Trees and bushes came within a few yards from the back entrance. The Club rooms were designed to allow as much undisturbed greenery as possible, allowing wild animals up close to the patio, where tourists could watch them. Six appreciated the Club owners for keeping it that way. It made his hunting job easier when he didn't have to jump over fences or carry equipment to cut through electric fences. He navigated around the pond with its Victorian water lilies, their large leaves spreading out like pads, and glowing green through the night googles. Bullfrogs croaked from the pond into the tranquil night.

Six was five minutes in, assessing the pattern of the guards, deciding on the best way to break into the cottage, when he sensed movement just in time to duck. Too late. The jab caught him on the jaw, barely missing the carotid. A blow meant to paralyze him.

"Crap!" Six groaned.

He shook his head, refocusing, before catching a flying kick to the gut that sent him down the creek slope, and planted his face in the mud. He heard the guards comment that it was probably an animal. He jumped to his feet and to the side as the assailant whizzed past him, high-kicking.

They squared off. His attacker was masked and hooded. He was a pro; the carotid blow was a pro move. Silent and deadly. But Six was also a full five inches taller than the assailant. He concluded this person was not part of the guard, otherwise he would have maimed Six, or captured him for interrogation, or killed him on the spot. His attacker wanted to end this quickly. Six spat on the ground. The attacker scrambled forward to him. Six blocked the blow and pinned the assassin to the ground, and pulled off the hood in one swoop.

"What? You!" Six said, loosening his grip.

The woman kneed his gut and tried to sit up.

"Dammit!" Six whispered. He squeezed again until the woman gulped for air. He let go of her and shoved her to the ground.

"What are you doing here?" Six said.

"What are you doing here?" the woman said, gasping and pulling her mask back on.

"What are you? I saw you hooking up with that guy at dinner."

"So you were nosing around? What makes you think I was hooking up with him?"

"Come on, even a crazy person can interpret that. You were all handsy with him at dinner. Like—"

"Like what?"

"Like you wanted him."

"The guy wanted someone to drink wine with and talk."

She was telling the truth, but Six wanted to hear any lies she might be using as part of her strategy. "I'm supposed to believe that?"

"Believe what you want."

"Those guys are dangerous."

"I know that."

Six brushed his jaw, which was hurting like hell. "You're definitely not a spoiled rich girl. What you did back there is the work of a pro. You almost broke my jaw."

"Stay out of my way!" Lin said. "I remember you," she said. "You were the guy in the lobby eyeing me the other day."

"I knew it. You were dressed like an anime character."

"What are you, CIA?"

"No."

"I know you are not with these guys, since you let me out of your grip."

"Maybe we are on the same side," Six said.

"That's subjective."

"Who are you with?"

"I'm a journalist."

"I'm supposed to believe that?"

"Believe what you want."

She sprinted away.

SEVENTEEN

SIX WOKE up before daybreak and completed his five-mile run. He decided to stop by the club café to grab a cup of coffee and some continental breakfast.

He noticed the woman at the coffee machine. He marveled at her transformation. She looked gorgeous—makeup, earrings, and bracelets, all well done. Ponytail that made her face symmetrical. And a straw hat on the table. Even in the safari khaki shirt, cargo shorts, and hiking boots, she looked attractive, revealing her toned legs. There were only four other people in the café.

She noticed Six entering the café and smiled as he approached her at the coffee bar.

"You survive on caffeine as well?" Six said.

Lin turned away while her coffee finished brewing. "You better stop talking to me."

"You're everywhere."

"So are you."

"This is the only place they have good coffee here."

"The room coffee tastes like crap."

"We both agree on that."

Six placed a Styrofoam cup into the niche and selected the latte option from the brewing machine.

"You're all suited up? Going out?" Six said.

"It's a safari, isn't it?"

"What are you doing here?"

"Getting breakfast. You're up so early yourself. Your face is healing well, I see."

He chuckled. "Good genes."

"I've a safari tour at seven."

"That's nice. I didn't get a memo for that one. I could have joined you."

"No."

"Why not? You're not the only one who likes to have fun."

"I have a date."

"A date? With whom?" Six said, wide-eyed. "Don't tell me."

"Yes, with him."

"The blob?"

"Shut up."

Six raised his hands in surrender.

"Enjoy your morning out with Mister Blob. He is a dangerous dude."

"You better eat your croissants and fruits. Your coffee is getting cold."

"Okay, date girl, I'm leaving now." Then Six wrote on a paper napkin and handed it to her.

"Meet us at the station tomorrow, at this address."

"I'll think about it. Now, go. My date is here."

Six remained stolid, watching the old man approach the coffee bar, followed by two of his bodyguards, who swept the room with their eyes.

She waved at the minister. The fat man looked flustered. He kissed her on the cheek.

"Good morning, my darling," he said.

"Good morning, Minister," Lin said.

"Please, darling. Just call me Nick. I insist," he said, in a gentle yet firm voice that resembled an underlying command. Who could blame him? The man was used to bossing people around, being a descendant of one of the continent's wealthiest families.

"Nick, this is—"

"George," Six interjected.

"George. We just met."

He shook his hand. "George?" he said with his shrewd piercing eyes, sizing Six up and down.

"Nice to meet you, Nick."

"American?"

"Yes," Six said, maintaining eye contact with the man, who seemed to be testing his strength. "I was on my way out."

The minister placed his hand on Lin's while maintaining eye contact with Six.

Six glanced at Lin. She smiled back. "See you around," said Lin.

Lin, the minister, and his men joined other tourists in the front lobby. Lin checked the several layers of makeup and mascara plastered on her face using the small mirror in her purse, something she had mastered as part of her job.

She had tried to hide the bruise on her cheek, but it still looked red and swollen.

"What happened to your face, my dear?" the minister said.

"Nothing."

"Really," he said, caressing her cheek.

"It's nothing," Lin said. "I drank a little too much and hit a doorframe and fell."

The minister looked unimpressed.

"Was it one of my men?"

"I fell."

"If ever one of my men raises a finger against you, let me know and I'll amputate their hand myself." He laughed, while his men remained silent and horrified.

Outside of the lobby, several Jeeps drove up for the tourists. The minister helped Lin into the car. "Here we go, my lady," he said.

"Thank you," she said. "Such a gentleman."

THE MORNING SAFARI WAS EVENTFUL, including several close contacts with Africa's Big Five animals and several rare birds, capped off by a sandwich and cold drink picnic around 9 a.m. near a waterhole with elephants, zebras, elands, and impalas. Nick was impressed with Lin's knowledge of wildlife and birds. They then headed back to the hotel and prepared for the day's official ceremony. Lin pinned on her press card.

Lin and the minister's entourage arrived at the orphanage learning center with great fanfare, just in time to do the ribbon cutting. His motorcade filled the small parking lot. Only his were new cars, four-by-fours. Each cost more money than all the school property combined. The only other car in the lot was the principal's beaten-up 1997 Volkswagen Golf.

The minister, who wore a sash and many medals, and Lin walked in side by side. The school principal, the mayor, and several respected community members all stood up and applauded. Everyone wore a t-shirt with the minister's face on it.

"It is true, then," Lin said, "that the people celebrate you here. I will report that."

He straightened himself.

"I'm impressed you're doing all this," Lin said.

"I love my community," he said, and beamed with pride.

"I can see that," Lin said, put off by the minister's self-glorification, given what she knew.

"One must give back. It's the least I can do."

"That's really generous of you."

The minister basked in the principal's and the mayor's extended praise for the minister's charity and love for young people, while Lin took notes.

"Is this a campaign?" she asked him.

"Sort of. But I do this because I want to."

Lin watched him smile and interact with the students. She liked that side of him.

CHAPTER
EIGHTEEN

REGGIE STOOD at the shelf deliberating which pack of gum to pick. She believed she had tried them all, but every time she came here, she wasted time deciding which one to get. She impulsively picked two packs, strawberry and watermelon flavors, and dropped them in the shopping basket. They gave her stomach gas, but they also helped her endure hours and hours of slow, methodical, and often boring scrutinizing of crime scenes, evidence, reports, and sometimes long drives. She carried her basket to the checkout line while still distracted by other items.

Reggie had been distracted when the cashier handed her a folded note.

It read: "I know who you are and leave this alone. If I were you, I would leave this area. People will die!" There was a smiley face after.

"Where did you get this?"

"The man who just left."

"Where?"

"There." She pointed towards the exit as the

man vanished around the corner. She glimpsed his brown leather jacket and that was all.

Shoot!

Reggie flung the grocery basket onto the counter and sprang towards the exit.

"Ma'am! You haven't paid yet!" the cashier shouted. Reggie ignored her.

She stood at the exit examining the throngs of people—locals, vendors with baskets on their head, and tourists.

She saw the man on the east side of the supermarket, then made a beeline towards that direction, striding but making sure to not cause panic. That side of the building was deserted, except for a few trees and a red dumpster. And the area was surrounded by a stone fence. *The man couldn't have jumped over the fence,* she thought. She clutched her gun just in case, her eyes locked on the trees for any sudden movement. This could be a trap. She tiptoed to the dumpster and heaved it open, gun drawn. "Police!" she said.

The young man sat in the dumpster, shaking. He had disheveled hair and unkempt clothes, and he stunk like hell, sitting in the slimy goo of rotting food. Reggie covered her nose and mouth momentarily before commanding the man to get out.

The man curled to the ground, protecting his face with his hands. "I don't know anything," he wailed. "Please don't hurt me!"

She studied the man. She quickly judged that he couldn't have written the note. He was probably high on drugs. Meth use had been trending up in parts of the country.

"I'm not going to hurt you. Who gave you this note?"

"Some man in a car. He said if I can give the gum-chewing lady this, he would give me money."

"Have you seen him before?"

"No."

She stared at him.

"Look, I know I'm shabby, but my mind is still sharp. I remember people I see."

"What's your name?"

"Louis."

"Louis, tell me what you saw."

"Like I said, the man called me to the car and said if I drop this note, he will give me dollars for food. And that's what I did."

"Why were you running?"

"I wanted to catch him before he left. Then I saw you running fast at me like a cop. I don't like cops. I got scared. I know what they do to people like me. This is all confusing."

"You don't get food from the supermarket?"

"Sometimes, I come here to get leftover food."

"Do you stay around here?"

"You can find me here every day."

Reggie handed him a two-dollar bill.

"Get some lunch and be careful of people you talk to."

"Yes. I will." The man smiled, showing his mouthful of stained teeth, his eyes shining for the first time.

Reggie walked away.

"Madam," he said.

Reggie paused and waited.

"I hear some things."

"What things?"

"Sometimes I go down to Chinatown. People say things in front of me because they think I'm stupid."

"What did you hear?"

"I heard some fellas talking about the missing kids."

"And?"

"They said the boss did it. They said the kids saw something they were not supposed to see."

"Are you sure?"

"I don't know the truth, but I'm sure of what I heard."

"They also said the boss is looking for something big in the falls."

"I know that—electricity."

"Something else, about immortality, electricity. That can make the old guy live forever."

"That makes little sense."

"That's what I heard. Thought I'd share. You were nice to me."

"Thanks, Louis. I will find you if I need more information."

"I will be here and there."

She thanked the man and rushed back into the store.

"I will need all the cameras from your store."

The cashier opened her mouth to say something, and stopped mid-sentence when Reggie displayed her badge.

"I'll tell the manager," she said, picking up the phone.

Reggie dialed her own phone.

"Hi, Reggie," Six replied, pleased that she had called.

"Meet me at the office in ten minutes!"

"Are you okay?"

"Just meet me there!"

"I'm on my way."

REGGIE BURST into the station and headed straight to the IT office. Seconds later, Six followed suit. Reggie explained to Six what had happened.

Clive entered the room moments later.

"What's going on?"

"Suspicious activity."

"So you told him, not me?"

"You're usually asleep at this time."

"Come on, I'm your partner. I was already here."

"Grateful you're here. Now let's do work."

The three sat and watched the black-and-white CCTV footage from the supermarket. Reggie fast-forwarded the video to the specific time point.

"There," she said, pausing the video. "That's a few minutes before Louis came into the store."

"Is that behind the store?" Clive said.

"Yes. It's the camera facing the dumpster," Reggie said.

"These guys don't have money for better cameras?" Six said.

Reggie laughed. "Every CCTV I've looked at is always crappy."

"It's so blurry, we can't even see his face," Six said.

"You can clearly see someone in a car rolling down the window, waving to someone," said Clive.

"That's Louis," Reggie said. "I can recognize that jacket. They talk for a bit, then he hands him a note, then the car disappears."

"He is a pro. Knew how to not get recognized. He never looks up."

"He knew where the cameras were."

"He also knew where I was."

"They did. Wonder how they knew."

Six thought for a moment.

"Might have a mole inside the station."

"You think so?" Clive said.

"These things tend to happen. In my experience, most crime rings usually have one or two cops in their pocket. I wouldn't be surprised."

"I guess we got to be careful whatever we discuss."

"I wouldn't trust anyone."

Reggie took a moment to think.

"You need to be careful from now on," Six said.

"I will not hide," Reggie said.

"I know you won't, but I want you to put me on speed dial."

"Okay."

"I'm your partner," Clive said in the native

language. "Why are you involving this American? He might be the mole."

"You know I can understand you, right?" Six said, staring at Clive.

Clive's face flushed.

Six rose and faced Clive. "Look, man, I'm just here until this thing is solved. You guys are short-handed for whatever we are against. Once this is done, I will be gone."

"Alright," Clive grumbled, and stormed out.

"What's wrong with that guy?" Six said.

"I think he is intimidated by you," Reggie said.

"I barely talk to him, or anyone for that matter. I just do my work."

"That's the thing. You're a mystery to him. And it scares some people. People like open books."

"Do I intimidate you?"

"No," she smiled. "I like to know the person first before I jump to conclusions. So far, you seem to me like someone that can be trusted."

"Alright. Let's go."

Reggie stopped by Clive's cubicle. Clive was startled when Reggie tapped him on the shoulder and said, "We are heading out to question a lead."

"Which one?"

"The park ranger."

"You think he might know something?"

"Not sure," she said, grabbing the car keys. "That's why we investigate, right? Anything is better than nothing at this point."

"Yeah, right," Clive said, nodding. "I'll just hang in here and do more of the paperwork."

Reggie sighed. "Alright. See you in a bit."

Six and Reggie exited the station.

CHAPTER
TWENTY

AFTER THE WINDING gravel roads riddled with potholes was the dirt road. They finally reached the property, where they were greeted by two shepherd dogs. They passed the cattle pen where three cows were tied to poles. There were three thatched huts, one evidently the kitchen, smoke whisking out through the thatched roof. The middle hut was round and much bigger, and the door was bolted with a chain and lock and paddle. Six guessed this was the storage. A woman was stomping grain with the *duri*, a tree trunk with a carved hollow center used for threshing grain. When she saw them, she stopped, stepped away from the tree trunk, welcomed them, and led them into the square thatched hut between the two. They sat on the fixed clay bench carved into the wall, forming a horseshoe around three walls. The stench of cow dung filled the room from the fresh dung plaster visible on the floor. A fire smoldered in the firepit. The room was so filled with smoke that Six felt he was running out of breath and sat next to the door. His eyes burned. It was very hot. With outside temperatures over 42 degrees Celsius, the fire made this room a furnace. He started sweating the moment he sat down. There were three people in the room—the safari ranger, who was named Conwell, and two young kids, a boy and a girl, half naked. The girl and boy were sitting on tree stumps, shelling drying corn into a basket. They looked at Six curiously. They all smiled at the visitors, while Conwell stood up and shook their hands.

The woman came in moments later with a basket full of ground cornmeal, which she added to the boiling water in the three-legged chrome pot on the fire. Then she stirred, using a wooden stick, in precise repeated circular motions until the pot's contents were thick. She then rolled up her long sleeves and forced the cooking stick back and forth while adding more cornmeal until the contents had thickened some more.

Six marveled at the wall, decorated with all their colorful plates and utensils. The children sat around a large basket, shelling corn with hands with such dexterity that it only took a few seconds to complete one cob. Reggie stood up and filled one of the straw baskets with dried corn on the cob, then started shelling. It was a job for women and children.

The couple passed pleasantries with Reggie, while Six marveled at how deftly they shelled the kernels from the cobs. In a matter of minutes, the wife had cooked their meal for them and presented it. Six wanted to refuse, but a look from Reggie told him to shut up.

They thanked the wife, washed their hands, and started eating. Mashed cornmeal with in-season vegetables, and tiny salty fish from the Beira Port in Mozambique. It tasted pretty good. Six knew that's all they had, but still they were generous. He admired such spirit.

They ate a little and thanked their hosts. After the little girl cleared the dishes and left-overs, the girl, the boy, and the wife went back outside to work.

"I have an older son," said Conwell. "He is working in Lusaka." Conwell proceeded to tell them all about his son. Six tried to be genial despite the heat and smoke. Thirty minutes later, when it was polite to do so, Reggie finally brought up the reason for the visit.

The safari ranger paused. He untied a fifty-kilogram sack kept behind the water containers. Tobacco smell filled the room. He then took out a few tobacco leaves from the sack, which he crumbled it into pieces using his hands, and spread onto a small piece of newspaper. Satisfied with the texture, he rolled the cigarette, expertly adding some saliva as glue. He picked a stick from the fire and lit the cigarette.

He took three deep puffs, each time letting out a long stream of white smoke.

"Oh, yes. The missing children," Conwell said, his face showing signs of concern. "I'll not forget that day."

"We know you were working guarding the youth hostel the day they disappeared."

"Yes, I was working. Like I always do every day. Same day as always. I knew something was not right."

"What happened?"

"The Club doesn't keep tabs on visitors even though signs are everywhere that warn and prohibit going into the jungle without a guide. On one of my rounds, I noticed some kids were not there. I woke up the neighboring boys and one of them said he had heard the other guys talking about going to the falls at night for a TikTok video."

"That's prohibited, right?"

Conwell nodded. "When I couldn't find them anywhere on the property, I took the path to the falls. I didn't think of telling my boss at the time because it was no big deal. I just had to find them."

Reggie and Six listened.

The man continued. "It was so dark. Minutes later I could hear voices and laughter near the Devil's Pool. From a distance, I could see they were taking selfies at the Devil's Pool."

Reggie and Six exchanged glances.

"We saw the videos," Reggie said.

"I didn't want to yell. The pool is at the edge of the falls before the drop. I didn't want to startle anyone in case they drop to their death."

The man shivered.

"Then a light and sound came, and they screamed before disappearing!"

"Light? A flashlight?"

"I've never seen anything like it."

Reggie looked at Six, then drew her iPhone from her pocket.

"Something that looked like this?"

Conwell scrutinized the image. "Yes, it looked like that. But again, I can't be sure. It was dark and it happened fast."

"You said they were attacked?"

"I don't know. I couldn't see."

"A crocodile?"

"That was something else—the roar. It was like a spirit. Evil. Then it all went blank."

Six looked at Reggie with skepticism.

"I see dangerous animals, lions, buffalo, venomous snakes. But this was something else. I woke up at the hospital. The last thing I remember is the light and rumbling noise."

"What do you think that was?"

"*Nyaminyami.* My grandmother used to tell us about it. I used to think it folklore back then."

"And now?"

"After what I saw, I think it's real."

Six and Reggie remained silent.

The man took another puff of his cigarette, then blew a stream of white smoke out.

"A lot of things have changed now after the new ownership. I'm not management, but I can tell when things are not straight."

"How so?" Reggie leaned in.

"They pay less money now. Going months without pay. Instead of having permanent positions, they laid off hundreds of people and now bring contract workers from the villages."

"Less liability on them."

"But the service has gone down now. They cut corners. That's why I was the only one on duty."

"You still look concerned," Reggie said.

"The boss is usually throwing parties with guys from the colliery company. And a lot of things happen and are said there."

"Such as?"

"I can't say."

"We are cops."

"The boss has every cop in this area in his pocket. He runs the P.D."

"We are not from this area."

This seemed to reassure him. "I used to be just a safari guide, but after the job cuts, I work more hours. So, when not guiding tourists, I work at the bar as a bartender, or as security. And when people are drunk, they say things they shouldn't say."

"What did you hear?"

"They bring in young girls, which I know is wrong, but what can I do? But last week, one of the visitors accidentally said something big was happening on Sunday."

"Specifics?"

"He asked me if I believed in immortality. I told him it was all mythology. Then he said many people were going to be in town to bid on the elixir of life. Millions of dollars."

"Sounds like drunk talk to me," Six said.

"His partner smacked him in the head and told him to be quiet. He was dead serious about it, not joking."

"Okay. We will be in touch." Reggie handed him her card. "Call us if you remember anything more."

The ranger nodded.

CHAPTER
TWENTY-ONE

COWS MOOED nearby as Six and Reggie climbed into the Jeep. Reggie burped. "Sorry!" she said, and guzzled water from the water bottle, and opened a pack of gum.

"It's all that salty fish," Six said.

"I know. It was a fantastic breakfast, though."

"You trust him?"

"He has a wife and three cows and kids. I don't see him messing around. He does his job. I think he saw something."

"How would only kids disappear, and he survives? The *Nyaminyami*? The immortality stuff? I can't wrap my mind around that."

"My gut tells me what he saw was serious," Reggie said. "It can't be coincidence that what Conwell said is the same as what Louis told me."

"I see your point. But what might 'the big happening this weekend' be?"

"That *Nyaminyami* story a good area to start.

Ask around about it. Wear a baseball hat, carry a brochure. They'll think you're a tourist."

"Okay."

"Say we meet at noon for lunch at the club café and go over our findings."

REGGIE ARRIVED at the club café a few minutes after noon. She smiled at Six.

"I apologize I'm late. African time."

"It's only ten minutes," Six said, smiling.

"A habit. Probably from growing up not caring what time it was."

"Good. I get to get another cup of coffee. It's zero calories."

"You worry about calories?" she said, marveling at his shredded arms.

"I do," Six smiled. "Discipline. Okay. What did you find out?"

"Most of what I found online was from a South African professor, de Klerk. Most of the research is from the eighties. He is an anthropology professor at the University of the Witwatersrand in Johannesburg. He has written extensively on African mythic literature and folklore, ranging from the Egyptians to the Zulu kingdom and everything in between," Reggie said.

"Anything interesting?"

"Most of his articles seem more superstition than the real analysis you would expect from an academic. He believed the *Nyaminyami* existed or might still exist, mainly from tales passed through oral tradition."

"That's all I heard from people at the Club. Stories. Nothing modern-day. I got a couple of lectures on 'Africans are not primitive.' Seems we are back to ground zero."

CHAPTER
TWENTY-TWO

REGGIE READ the news on the morning newspaper's front page while grabbing gum and a snack at a neighborhood kiosk. She ran to the station and then phoned Six, drove over, and picked him up ten minutes later at the Club foyer.

"Louis is dead!" Reggie said, with teary eyes. "Officers on duty talking about some druggie found dead, and the paper said it was Louis."

They drove to the flea market where Louis's body had been found near the dumpster. People were going about their days as usual in a place where someone had died a few hours earlier.

"Were there any officers around?"

"No," Reggie said, showing anger in her voice. "The station here is understaffed, and they couldn't care less for a druggie dying in the streets. Less stuff to worry about. They couldn't care less about expending resources on a street person, unless a relative was breathing down their neck demanding justice."

"So the assumption is he died of drugs?"

"That's what the preliminary office report said."

"Who was the officer on duty?"

"Jim."

"Did you talk to him?"

"No. He didn't even go to the scene."

They drove a few kilometers in silence.

"Hey," Six said. "It's not your fault. Before yesterday, you didn't even know this guy."

"He's dead because of me."

"You don't know that."

"Hell, I do. Whoever gave him the note came back to finish the job. They want me."

"You can't be sure."

"I will find that son of a bitch who was in the video."

"I'm sure if there is something, we will sort this out."

"When I talked to Louis yesterday, he kept murmuring that something was going down. He kept saying that over and over until I gave him a two-dollar bill."

"Maybe he was just insane."

"Louis was adamant that the guards were talking about it."

"Eternal life again?"

"I know it sounds like bullshit. Many people still believe in finding the elixir of life. Plus, two people now have mentioned something to that end."

"Yeah, a 'something' we can't even define. How do you get evidence for that? There is orange tape everywhere, and Vic Falls is swarming with security now, guarding the equipment. My water samples turned up nothing."

"I will get a search warrant."

"Search where? Search what? Without probable cause? Based on some crazy guy's hearsay?"

"What else would one need to do to get actual information and history?"

"Somebody this morning told me to talk to the elders, the witch doctors, they know stuff, oral tradition passed down for generations."

"That is what they say to Americans."

"I say we start there. Doesn't hurt. I mean, I would like to learn about this place before the Europeans came and gave us their version of history."

"First, to the morgue."

By now they had reached the Victoria Falls regional hospital, its southern campus. Reggie parked the car.

"You stay here," she told Six.

"You might need backup," Six said.

"I already have an official partner," Reggie said, "and if they see me with anybody it should be him."

"I know this is not your M.O., but if you're going to crack this, don't you think more hands might be better? Plus, there are so many angles to this. You know the locals and I don't. But I also have access to resources that can be helpful."

Reggie looked at him for a few moments in silence.

"You know this is dangerous, and you don't get paid."

"I work alone under dangerous conditions. I'm happy to help as much as I can. And I know you'll have my back."

They both smiled.

Reggie reached into her pocket and handed Six a laminated badge.

"What's this?"

"I'm hiring you as a contract private investigator. This makes things easier."

"It's legal?"

"In this case, it is."

"Who else knows about your encounter with Louis?" Six said.

"The store cashier, you, me, and Clive," Reggie said.

"We need to talk to the cashier."

"I already sent guys to get her."

"Good."

"But first, the morgue."

CHAPTER
TWENTY-THREE

THEY PASSED through the glass front doors into the lobby, lined with patients waiting to get help. Reggie cut the line to the front, as the irritated eyes of tired patients bored through her. The woman behind the counter was about to chide her when Reggie flashed her badge.

"Detective Thandiwe Kona," Reggie said. "And my partner Six. We are here to see the medical examiner."

The woman scrutinized Six. She picked up the telephone and dialed. Seconds later, she said, "Corridor to your right."

The medical examiner met them halfway along the corridor. A petite, cheerful woman, shook both Reggie and Six's hands.

"Joyce, this is my partner Six."

"Where did you get him?" Joyce said, eyeing him.

"We're just partners for a bit, for this case."

"I like him already better than your other partner."

The large room with the steel sink was slightly warm and smelled of decomposing human flesh. Six and Reggie wrinkled their noses.

"That's what you get with so much load shedding," said Joyce.

"They ration electricity to hospitals as well?"

"Of course," Joyce said. "Ours is a government hospital, and as you can tell, our clientele is not filthy rich, relying mostly on free services. And nothing free is ever first-class in this world."

"How do you get used to this smell?" Reggie said under her breath.

"You don't. You just do it. If I don't do it, who will? This way," said Joyce, unlocking a pair of beige metal doors.

They followed her.

"The summer temperatures make it bad. Especially when you have members with no I.D., and we must identify them before they can be released. Same with your friend you're going to see."

"Who told you he is my friend?" said Reggie, sharply.

"What happens if they stay here long, unclaimed?" Six cut in.

"Cremation. That's our only option. If you had been here a day later, he would be ash by now."

An even stronger smell pervaded this room. They watched while Joyce read the tags attached to the trays lined on the wall, before finally pulling one farther to the right.

"Here you go!" she said. She rolled the tray

onto the examination bed and opened the bag. Six and Reggie approached, examining the dead man. His body had been surgically bisected, then sewn together with visible zigzag patches. His skin was pale dark, eyes bulging from the sockets, mouth wide open, lips gripping at the stained teeth. He looked as if he could scream at any moment. It was clear from the man's facial expression that his last living encounter had not been pleasing. A chilling stare.

"I examined him last night when he came in. There were visible signs of struggle." She lifted the man's forearm. Then Joyce continued, "Apart from that, seems like a typical overdose."

"But he told me he didn't use that. Said he had been clean for many years," Reggie said.

"You believed him?"

"Yes."

"Overdose."

"Confirmed?"

"We have to wait for the laboratory results." Joyce rolled the body back into the tray. "I've examined several teenagers dead from the same drug within the last several months. The numbers have surged since last August, unlike we've seen before."

"That's the same time construction was commissioned for the hydro-power plant."

"Yes," Joyce said.

Six said, "So the project brought drugs to this area?"

"You have people across Africa and Asia working here. They spend money on drugs, or they deal in them."

"Where do they get the drugs?"

"People say from the prefab Chinatown. The people there make it and sell it."

"Was he wearing a brown leather jacket?"

"If there was," said Joyce, "somebody took it."

They thanked Joyce and left the hospital.

"All these things are connected," Six told Reggie in the car. "I am going there tonight to find some answers."

"Why are you going there? We don't have time."

"A hunch. Nothing to lose."

CHAPTER
TWENTY-FOUR

THE CASHIER, whose name was Plaxecedes, sat hunched on the other side of the table in the interrogation room, her expression a mixture of confusion and frustration. Reggie and Clive entered the room.

She looked up, recognizing Reggie. "Can someone tell me why I am here?"

"We have a few questions for you," Reggie said.

"Is this about the note? I don't know anything. I told you to ask Louis. He is the one who gave me the note!"

"Louis is dead," Reggie said.

Plaxecedes shivered in her chair as her face turned pale, as if she had just seen a ghost.

"Someone found his body by the dumpster behind the flea market."

"That's horrible! What? That can't be true."

"It is," Reggie said, and paused for a moment, letting the news settle.

"Ma'am, is there anything you're not telling us?"

"No, I told you everything."

"If you lie, that's life in prison for withholding evidence from the police for a murder. Obstruction of justice."

"I swear I know nothing."

"I believe you," Reggie said. "But I'm sure you understand why we have you here."

"Yes," she said, now a little settled. "I handed you the note."

"Correct."

They waited, letting her gather her thoughts.

"Anything you can give us will help."

"I see hundreds of people every day. Buses with visitors stop there for lunch."

"How long have you been working at the store?"

"Four years."

"Anything like this happened before?"

"My customers being murdered?"

"I mean Louis giving you notes."

"I thought nothing of it when he gave me this one. I didn't make anything of it. I was so busy working alone."

"Can you tell us more about Louis?"

"What do you want to know?"

"Anything."

"Sometimes good people go through hard times," she said, her eyes filling with tears. "He was a frequent in the store. And he was one of the nicest customers. In my work you meet all kinds of mean people who often treat us like we're nothing."

"Did you ever talk to him more?"

"Not much, but I could tell that man would not harm a fly!"

"Why do you say that?"

"I am a mother. He is the age of my son. I think it was six months ago when we started seeing a man sleeping behind the store. I didn't like it at first, but the manager gave it some time to see if he would move on."

"And?"

"He was always respectful. Never caused any harm. He even stood up for me when a bunch of teenagers were causing trouble, trying to record a video in the store. And even stopped some vagabonds from setting fire."

"Did he use drugs?"

"Like I said, he was the nicest person I've ever met. I even gave him some money for a small job to sweep and clean the front of the store each morning." She smiled, looking blankly into the air. "He would pick up all the trash even throughout the day."

"So you believe he didn't use any drugs?"

"Louis? No. I'd have known. I see a lot of kids use drugs nowadays, but Louis, I've never seen him high. Trust me. A lot of them come through the store high on that drug, triple Z, that's what they call it on the streets. I know when someone is high."

Reggie waited.

"I believe he didn't because he used the money we paid him to buy food from our store, and clothes."

"So you knew him well?"

"No, but I liked him as a gentleman. You wouldn't believe the disrespect I get from people who come through the store. That poor man. Over the months, I would give him leftover food at the end of the day. We trash the food anyway. What a waste!"

"That explains why he came to you with the note."

"Maybe. I don't know why he gave it to me." Reggie sighed.

"Can you think of anything else? Anything you might have seen or heard. Anything Louis might have told you?"

"No."

"Okay. Do you have any relatives where you and your family could lie low for a few weeks?"

"I have a sister in Plumtree. Why?"

"We believe whoever killed Louis might come after you as well, thinking you know something."

Her eyes opened wider with panic. "I'm just a cashier. Oh, God! I haven't hurt anyone."

"We believe you, but these people might not."

She covered her face with her palms. "I know nothing."

"They might not care. I'm sure Louis knew nothing too. They may think Louis told you some information. They will try to tie loose ends."

"I've children. All I do is work to provide for my family."

"I suggest you visit your sister for a few weeks while we solve this."

"It's not month end yet. I don't have any money."

"How much does it cost to get there?"

"One hundred and fifty dollars for three people, I'd say."

Reggie opened her billfold and handed her one hundred and fifty dollars.

"What about my work?"

"Ask for sick leave. Do not tell anyone where you are going."

Plaxecedes was dismissed. Reggie sat deep in thought.

"How did the officer on duty hear about Louis?" Reggie said.

"Anonymous tip," Clive said.

Because Reggie seemed unconvinced, Clive said, "Are you thinking officers might be involved?"

"No," Reggie said. "What I'm trying to solve is why not just kill the guy and dump him in the river. Make him disappear? Whoever did this wanted us to know about it."

"A drug overdose is plausible," Clive said.

"I think there's more to this. Let's be careful," Reggie said.

"Care to share?"

"I will find out."

CHAPTER
TWENTY-FIVE

"WE NEED to talk to the mayor about the drug issue," Six said to Reggie and Clive.

"That man is untouchable," Clive said. "We really have nothing to nail him to the wall."

"He has every cop in town in his pocket. Any allegations will go to nothing," Reggie said.

"What about the guy named Liu? Last time I saw them, he looked like the mayor's right-hand man."

"He is. He does the dirty work for them. He runs Chinatown."

"How do you know?" Six said.

"Everyone who lives here knows," Clive said. "The new colliery is all his, in exchange for keeping laborers from troubling the mayor."

"Is there a way to get to Liu?"

"You can't. He is invincible. His place is guarded 24/7. When he's out, he usually has a couple of guards with him," Clive said.

"If the mayor visit doesn't work out, we could pay Liu a visit?" Reggie said.

"I cannot see getting access to him."

Six said, "Nothing at this point is useless. We need any lead we can get."

Moments later, Clive joined Reggie and Six in the car, grudgingly taking the back seat.

Reggie flashed her badge to the three guards at the municipal building's front gate. The men scrutinized the badge, then one spoke into his walkie. He pushed the metal gate open.

They parked the Jeep among several expensive SUVs. The receptionist talked on the phone and directed them to the elevator.

The mayor's office was on the third floor, directly opposite the elevator, overlooking the main street. A wall plaque mounted to the right of the door read: Mayor Gideon Hove. The door was slightly open, as he had been expecting them.

"Come on in," the man said.

They exchanged pleasantries, and the mayor bragged about incoming big-money investments and a few developments underway in town.

"Obviously, you all didn't come here to chitchat, so let's get on with it," the mayor said.

Reggie looked at both Six and Clive, then spoke.

"Mr. Mayor, we have reason to suspect there is some organized crime in the city that started after the approval of the hydro-power project."

The man's warm features vanished. He steepled his hands.

"So I've heard. Do you have any evidence for these claims?"

"Yes," Reggie showed him the newspaper

clip about Louis. He gave it one glance and smirked. "That guy was a druggie. That's why he was homeless."

"That's what the report says," Reggie said. "We have seen cases of drug overdose death skyrocketing over the past year."

"Do we know where the drugs are coming from?"

"Foreign labor brings its vices, and imports are not a municipal issue."

"We suspect it's from Chinatown."

"You think the project manufactures drugs here."

"Yes."

"What do you suggest I do?"

"Increase police surveillance in the area. Especially merchandise going out to schools."

"Our force is already understaffed."

"I understand, sir, but if we can prevent the source of the drugs, then we can save the money the city is losing dealing with deaths from drugs."

The mayor seemed to deliberate for a moment. Then he said, "That will be hard, if not impossible. This company has brought millions of dollars into the town. One clause in the contract was to let them do their job without too much interference."

"We let kids continue to overdose over some clause in the contract?" Reggie said.

"It's nothing compared to the revenue it has brought to the city. Improved roads, a world-class shopping center. Money is flowing in. We can't complain. Look around you."

"Sir—?"

"We can't just invade the area with too many cops. That will raise eyebrows, and God knows we need all the foreign investment. I will talk to the police chief. But I don't think because one druggie dies, you make it suddenly an epidemic. I'd suggest you use your resources elsewhere. Focus on finding the missing tourists."

"Yes, sir," Clive said.

The mayor checked his cellphone.

"If you'll excuse me, I've an important meeting with the city developers. Let me know when you have concrete evidence of anything."

CHAPTER
TWENTY-SIX

AT THE STATION CLIVE SAID, "Guys, I think we are wasting time. I don't see a connection between a drug user's death and the missing kids."

Six looked at Reggie. "Care for a quick ride into town?"

"Sure, why not? We might get something useful, like coffee."

"Is anyone listening to what I just said?" Clive said.

Reggie patted him on the shoulder. "Take it easy. He just has a different way of finding answers. We are on the same team, remember?"

Clive did not answer.

The flea market at this hour was packed. The area was divided into two sections: one side fresh produce, the other side everything else, ranging from used clothes in bales, shoes, gadgets, electronics—mostly Chinese products. Vendors lined the streets trading in roasted corn, chips, ice cream, roasted birds on sticks. Reggie and Six squeezed past to the food court across the street. Most of the people were dining inside. Mounds of fries, pizza, and fried chicken. All western junk. Six noticed that most people preferred this. The trend, a plague. Sugar, salt, and fat. All the pop-up pizza and fried-chicken restaurants congested near bus stops. Despite evidence that obesity was a recipe for a shorter life span, and countless media outlets showing that obesity had overtaken communicable disease as the major killer, overtaking AIDS, malaria, and cholera combined, people still wanted to eat. Interestingly for Six, fat here was beautiful. Every girl wanted to be big—big thighs, big chest, big butts. Men likewise. The inability to see one's belt buckle meant you lived like the rich.

An hour later, they sat in the Jeep riding towards Reggie's bed-and-breakfast, having learned nothing fruitful towards solving the case. No one at the flea market had provided useful information. However, Reggie had negotiated her way to several bundles of cheap fresh vegetables and leafy greens.

At Reggie's they both cooked.

"I like to cook," Six said.

"Your mama teach you?"

"I've always lived by myself since a young age. My parents died in a car crash when I was nine."

"I'm sorry. What happened?"

"Drunk driver," he said. "Ironically, the drunk guy survived."

"That's sad."

"It was. But I guess that taught me some self-reliance."

Six watched Reggie prepare *sadza*. First, she boiled water, then added cornmeal until it was thick enough. On the other stove plate, Six diced the tomatoes and added the vegetables into a vegetable stew. Reggie made the okra. Boiled, with light spice.

Twenty minutes later, they sat at the table on the porch. One bowl with the *sadza*, one bowl with the vegetables, and the third bowl with the okra soup.

"Are we eating from the same plate?"

"That's how we do it here, traditionally," Reggie said, smiling.

Six nodded.

"Hands only," Reggie said, when Six fumbled around for a spoon.

"Then how do you eat the okra?"

"I'll show you."

Six observed while Reggie grabbed a piece of the *sadza*, rolling it in her hands until it was a bolus, well rounded, then, using her thumb, she formed a depression on the bolus which she then dipped into the okra soup. She moved her hands in a circular motion allowing the slimy okra strands to break, then chewed the whole thing.

Six did the same.

"This is great!" he said.

"I told you."

CHAPTER
TWENTY-SEVEN

LIN CHECKED the napkin with the phone number from Six. She wondered how the paper had found its way into her cargo pocket. She read the number out loud. She threw the rest of her clothes into the washing machine and started it. She hurried to the Club's gym and completed a sixteen-minute 5K on the treadmill, then topped that with some intense plyometrics. She took a cold shower and changed into brown slacks and hiking boots. She never knew where she would end up, so she wore the boots, just in case.

She called Six and told him to meet her alone in town. They agreed to meet at a coffee shop a few blocks from the Safari Club.

The place was bustling with patrons.

"Thanks for agreeing to meet with me here," she said.

"Of course. I'm happy to," Six said.

"I don't trust local cops and don't want to

jeopardize all my work with the minister," she said.

"Smart move, choosing this place. The public outdoor restaurant."

They sat outside, overlooking a portion of the falls, watching tourists and locals window-shopping and strolling along the cobbled streets. Six ordered a mocha and a chocolate croissant. Lin ordered red tea with a cream-cheese danish.

"I'm British and Japanese," she explained.

"Makes sense."

"I'm kidding. I just like tea in the afternoon."

Six waited while she added several teaspoons of sugar.

"Is George your real name?"

"Yes."

"Right? Try again. What are you? I'm guessing a mix of English and German."

Six smiled. "Yours?"

"Okay, let's start afresh. I'm Taki Shu-Lin."

"Should've guessed," Six said, pointing at the Naruto manga character tattooed on her neck.

"Yeah. I'm a big fan. Your name?"

"Six."

"Nice to meet you, Six. You going to tell me your real name?"

"Draye Sixpence. People who know me just call me Six."

"Nice to meet you."

"You were saying you think there's something?" Six said.

"I'm starting to connect the dots."

"Be careful," Six said. "If the guy is who we think he is, he is dangerous."

"So now you're worried about me? What a gentleman," Lin said, twirling her hair. "I may not look like I can, but I can stand my ground."

"I know you can. I am serious."

"Nick was a little jealous the last time he saw me talking to you at breakfast. That's why we met here."

"You're kidding?"

"I'm not," she said. "He's probably used to getting what he wants. But for me it's different."

"Did you tell him we were hooking up?"

She seemed unbothered by this. "You were there. I told him I had just met you."

"And?"

"Later he asked me what I thought about you. I told him I thought you were hot. I didn't lie. You are handsome. If I must get a man's trust, I must tell him the truth. Even he knows that."

Lin took a sip of her tea while Six bit into the croissant, catching flakes with a paper towel.

"Plus, that kind of throws him off his game a little. Now he has to flex everything he has."

"I see. That's why you guys are going on safaris?"

"Yes. The man likes to brag," she said. "Plus, it's good to be in the sun. I need all the Vitamin D I can get." She wanted to add, "after spending weeks in a container," but did not.

"So what are you? His trophy girl. I mean—"

She kicked him in the shin.

"I deserved that," Six said.

"He probably has some guy following me around and watching me right now."

Lin explained to Six how she had infiltrated the human trafficking ring, which had led her here to Victoria Falls in a cargo tank with twenty other girls.

"That is crazy!" Six said when Lin had finished.

"I arrived with them a few days ago. Then we were separated. I've been trying to locate where we were unloaded, but they are smart to keep their tracks underground."

"Any leads?"

"One person who would know is the mayor."

"How?"

"He runs this place. And he's close to the minister. Nothing and nobody goes in or out without him knowing. If we can get to him, we might get answers."

"We already asked."

"From your face, I guess it was useless?"

"Waste of time. He didn't give a crap. The guy only answered our questions with more questions. And seemed like he was expecting us."

"I think it will take a little more than questioning to make him give you the answers."

Six looked at her.

"Do you think it will put you in danger if the minister finds out I'm working with cops?" she said.

"I think he already knows by now. If not, he is already looking. I'm sure he will find nothing."

"How do you know?"

"I looked you up. And I don't mean google. My guys couldn't find anything on you. Clean."

"I work for MI6," Lin said. She observed Six's face. He seemed unfazed.

Lin explained that she was a British MI6 agent, sent to investigate the contractor suspected of human-trafficking crimes. "Wanted for crimes across four continents. Been on his tail for four years and I wouldn't want you to jeopardize this mission."

"Thought Britain left Zimbabwe many years ago."

"Yeah, we did, but we still run the country. Our extractive systems are still in place. Only difference is instead of a white man running the show, now there are black puppets who carry out the deeds. Like a front. We buy all the diamonds, gold, and plenty of minerals as ore, for peanuts compared to what we get when refined."

"There are fine engineers here. I always wondered why the country doesn't build their own manufacturing industries to refine and process raw material. They would earn more for the dollar."

"It's hard to break instilled habits. The notion of dependency has been forged into their minds for centuries, and the few guys in power hoard whatever comes. Kickbacks, corruption, human trafficking, and more. We think the minister has been trafficking girls and child laborers all over Africa. And African girls go to China. There's a shortage of women there. Some of his conspirators from Nigeria are in jail, but this guy has been elusive. And they have expanded to

Asian countries to meet the demand for thousands of temporary workers in Africa."

"Since when did your government start caring about human trafficking?"

"I should be asking you," she said.

"If it were guns and drugs, we would already be all over this guy."

"Sad, but true. Trafficking has been on the back burner."

"Why did you ask to meet me?" Six said.

"You left a note."

"I did. I was worried about you hanging out with the minister. That was before I knew who you are."

Lin remained quiet and took a sip of her tea.

Six continued. "It's been big business way before I was born. Last I checked, MI6 and all these agencies didn't give a damn about it unless it was drugs or weapons. When did they start caring about little girls or boys in containers?"

"They do now."

"Must be very personal for you."

"Judging so much, why are you here?"

"I'll know more soon."

"Really? We can play this game all day."

"We are the guys who clean up for countries."

"Contractor?"

"My covert organization."

"What exactly do you clean up?"

"Illegal activities. Organized crime. Shell companies. Kickbacks, mineral theft, money laundering, materials used for illicit purposes, and crimes like that."

Lin nodded. "Development is just a front for unscrupulous activities."

"There's more," Six said. "Your guy purchased a multimillion-dollar beachfront mansion in Florida."

"How did you dig that up? It's not lying in plain sight."

"The people I work for have some of the best resources and manpower in the world. More than many governments. And they are good at what they do. Digging through cash trails and shell companies wouldn't be impossible to do."

"Why the sudden trust in sharing your mission?"

"Why not?"

"You're not afraid I'll divulge it?"

"No."

"Why?"

"Instinct."

"You trust me?"

"I don't. But if I didn't trust you, I could have killed you. And you could have killed me likewise. But you didn't. I believe we are on the same mission."

"The feeling is mutual."

CHAPTER
TWENTY-EIGHT

SIX AND REGGIE spent the rest of the day going over reports and logs of all employees at the Safari club. Everyone was still around. It was the busiest season. All employees available that night were summoned to the dining area where the police went about interviewing them. Everything lined up. Variable answers, non-helpful.

Next, they had gone to the station and reviewed the footage retrieved from the cloud and reviewed the footage posted on social media by one of the missing kids. He was a known vlogger, usually posting about doing dangerous feats, jumping off cliffs and paragliding at exotic locations around the world. It got even more colorful when he began to film with drones.

"Look at all the stuff they do," Reggie said, scrolling down videos on the vlogger's channel.

"That's some crazy stuff," Six said.

"I wonder if their parents are cool with all this."

"Entitled millennials, they don't care."

"Who in their right minds takes selfies at the Devil's Pool?"

"Kids. They enjoy doing crazy things now. Those days of decency are gone."

"But nature always wins one way or the other."

"We mess up the climate, we suffer. We mess up with the wild, we suffer!"

They continued looking through the videos for clues.

Six leaned back in the chair. "Where is your partner?" Six said.

"Haven't seen him. Probably passed out in some brothel. Not a first, though."

"How do you work with this guy?" Six said.

"I've learned to suffer fools gladly."

"That takes special character and patience."

"I hope he gets around to himself soon. He used to try to be a good cop."

"Isn't he married?"

"He is," she said. "Feel bad for the wife. Stays home in the rural taking care of the kids while he is getting filthy here."

"Not worried about diseases, HIV and all? That stuff is rampant in these parts!"

"God knows I tried. Even used threats. Some people only learn when they get it."

"Never tolerate people whose primary goal is to constantly pull you down to their level. Especially those with no remorse, and don't want to change their ways. Before you know it, you start believing you too are just a chicken, not an eagle! Life is a beautiful thing that ought to be celebrated by believing in the good in others, while having the discernment to know when not to be used by others for their own narcissism."

"Preach on, partner." Reggie slapped him on the shoulder.

Six rewound the vlogger's video.

He looked more closely. "Hold on. I know this one kid!" Six said.

"From where?"

"I met them three days ago, the night I got here. The family and I shared a dinner table. His name is Jadin. Seemed like such a cool kid, played football. Planning to go pro."

"The video already has millions of views and reshares."

"Scary, but no one knows if it's real or not. Nowadays social media is littered with fake videos."

"I know. AI and advanced editing software makes it almost impossible to spot a manipulated video from a real one."

Six leaned in closer to the screen.

"Turn up the volume, slow it down. Do you hear that?"

They listened.

"Do you hear the sound?" Six said.

"Like an engine."

The merry voices turned distressed before the camera crashed into the rocks. Everyone was in a dither. Then everything became a bright blank.

"That lines up with what the safari guide said—the light and loud sound."

"He was right."

"I've been thinking about what he said," Six

said. "The immortality thing. What if it's the truth? I know it sounds nuts."

"No, not at all. I'm African, remember. We do believe in some superstition."

"That story and the missing kids may be linked. What if the kids had seen whatever this immortality thing is? And someone shut them up."

"There is no way to prove that."

Six stood up and walked back and forth. "Let's consider, if it was real, how we would go about finding that out."

"Would be easier if we had found the remains."

"I think it's a good thing we didn't. May mean the kids are still alive."

"Then we have to find them."

"What else could we do to corroborate the safari guide's story?"

"It's hearsay, we can't corroborate that."

"Professor de Klerk at the University of the Witwatersrand in Johannesburg is an anthropologist—"

"But you already talked to him."

"Only by email. I need to interview him in person."

"I'll get another air ticket and come with you. I've unlimited sky miles, so no big deal."

"You must travel a lot."

"Perks for the job. Comes in handy in times like these."

"Let's do it," she said.

"Done."

CHAPTER
TWENTY-NINE

SIX AND REGGIE stayed at the office till after 5 p.m. Reggie stepped outside and returned with two water bottles. Six leaned back in the chair with his legs propped on another chair, his hands interlaced behind his head.

"What's up?" Reggie said. She handed one water bottle to Six.

Six sat up straight. "There's something that makes little sense," Six said. "Why isn't this place swarming with cops, the FBI, or the press? American kids missing and it all plays underground? What parent would be silent when their kids disappear?"

"The parents didn't want that. They demanded it stay low key. They don't want all the media pressure."

"Did you talk to them?"

"No. Their statement was taken before I got here. I just went over the report yesterday. Apparently, the father is a majority shareholder in the hydro-power project. That's why the higher-ups send us. They wanted the best looking into this. They have been giving us hell."

"Why would they want to keep it under wraps when their kids are missing?"

"Business interests I suppose," Reggie said. "The hydro-power project has faced intense op-position. Anything could be a reason to shut down the entire operation. Just imagine how much international fuss that would create. The parents still believe the kids are alive. The press will be their last resort."

"We should talk to them. They might have a role in this. They didn't call the embassy or threaten to sue the Safari Club. What parent would do such a thing?"

Reggie thought for a second.

"I see your point. I was planning to talk to them after getting through what we have. They are still staying at the Safari Club. The earlier the better."

"Let's go."

THEY REACHED the Safari Club few minutes later. The concierge called the Bileses' room and told Six to go left to suite 24.

Reggie rang the doorbell once. Mr. Biles opened the door. She recognized his face from the reports.

"Mr. Biles. Detective Thandiwe Kona and my partner Six."

Reggie flashed her badge.

"Detective. You reputation precedes you." He extended his hand, which Reggie shook.

Mr. Biles' eyes widened, recognizing Six.

"I thought your name was James," Mr. Biles said.

"It's complicated," Six said.

"Well, nice to meet you, again, Six."

"You know each other?" Reggie said.

"Yes. We shared a dinner table two nights ago," Six said.

"Small world."

Mr. Biles looked at Six. "I didn't realize you were a cop."

"I… I'm not. Just helping."

They followed the man past the kitchen to the living room, where his wife sat on the couch, wrapped in a throw. Two empty bottles of scotch lay empty on the coffee table next to two half-empty glasses. A tray with untouched breakfast was on the dining table. Mr. Biles pointed to two chairs opposite the couch and plopped down next to his wife. Reggie and Six sat down. His wife never lifted her head to look at the visitors.

"Any news for us?" Mr. Biles said.

"No, sir. Our team is still looking," Reggie said.

"Then why are you here?"

"We have a few more questions," Six said.

"What can we help you with? We already gave statements to the previous cops."

Mrs. Biles lifted her head for the first time. Her eyes were red and puffy, her cheeks red.

"We found nothing. No remains."

"That's a good thing, isn't it," Mr. Biles said

"It is."

"My babies! Find my babies!" the wife said. There were no tears. She had cried enough.

Reggie held Mrs. Biles' hand to comfort her.

"Mrs. Biles. We are doing the best we can. I promise you we will do everything in our power to bring you kids back."

She looked at Reggie and said nothing.

Her husband rubbed her back. They waited until his wife finished wailing.

"What do you want to know?" Mr. Biles said.

"If I may ask, why didn't you report this to the embassy or the press?" Six said.

"No, not the press. We don't want the pressure. We don't want to create a big fuss about this until we are certain."

"Does it seem odd that your kids disappeared together?"

"No, not really. Our kids have always been inseparable. They do most things together, you know. They compete in sports, basketball, soccer. I guess being the only siblings, they have always been close."

"Has anyone contacted you about your kids?"

"No. Why?"

"Mr. Biles," Six said. "I understand you are a major investor in the hydro-power project. Do you think it's connected to your children disappearing?"

"No. I am a businessman, but I would never put my family in danger."

"Can you think of someone who would want to hurt you or your kids?"

The wife looked at the husband.

Mr. Biles spoke. "No, I can't think of anyone who would want to hurt us. But I'm a successful businessman. And haters are everywhere. We try to treat everyone with integrity, and lie low as much as we can."

"You never know. These things happen," Reggie said.

The wife looked up. "Are you suggesting they were kidnapped?"

"No. We are just looking at all the angles. Anything helpful."

"Anything else?" Mr. Biles said.

"No. Thank you for your time."

They thanked the Bileses and strode towards the door. Mr. Biles walked them to the door.

He looked Reggie in the eye.

"Detective, I put my trust in your team. Don't disappoint me. Do it for my wife. Find our kids." He turned and looked at his wife, who still sat slumped on the couch.

"I understand, sir. We will be in touch."

They walked out.

"Do you trust him?" Six said to Reggie while they walked to the car.

"I don't know yet. Part of me does, part of me doesn't."

"Why do you say so?"

"Did you see how stoic he was. The man is as calm as anyone I've ever seen in his situation. I understand. Maybe he is staying strong for the wife."

"Might be from experience. He is a business guy. I'm sure he is used to taking nerve-wrecking risks."

"Do you believe him?"

"I don't know either. Time will tell."

LIN WAITED in the welcome area. Nick had promised her a surprise. She checked her watch. It was already dusk, close to 6 p.m., and the sun was sinking toward the western horizon.

Nick arrived fifteen minutes later. He kissed her hand.

"You're punctual, my dear."

"I didn't want to miss the surprise."

Four other men in khakis joined them. She could tell two were American, one British, and one most likely Dutch, from their accents. The guide arrived several minutes later with a truck, which the group boarded. The back of the truck was loaded with specialty hunting rifles and crossbows.

"What is this for?"

"Hunting," Nick said. "Oh, man, this is going to be fun!"

Lin looked at the other men, who all smiled back.

"Jack, do you think we have a chance of seeing lions today?" Nick asked the driver.

"The boss had us drop some carcasses in one area, so the beasts should be there, sir."

The Dutch man spoke. "They better be there. I paid a shit ton for this."

It grew dark, and the two headlights shone the way through the narrow jungle road.

"You didn't tell me it was hunting," Lin said.

"That would have ruined the surprise. Are you scared?"

"I don't like seeing animals abused."

"Relax. This will be the most intense feeling you will ever feel. Taking down the king of the jungle. Only one of us, who does the killing shot, can take the prize home."

"So is this trophy hunting?"

"You say it like it's a bad thing."

"It is. Who kills animals for sport?"

"These guys have fun, and the country gets foreign currency."

"Do the locals benefit?"

The minister deliberated, then said, "Of course, they do. They get jobs."

"What do you hunt for?"

"Lions! Any of the Big Five."

Lin cringed.

"You haven't felt the rush of adrenalin when you nail a bull. Watch the king of the jungle fall in your crossbow's scope. There is nothing like that feeling."

The truck stopped and shut off the lights.

"Okay, gentlemen and lady," the driver said. "From now, you're on foot. Your emergency beacon is on your sleeve. Just press that if you need help. Stay safe. We meet here at eight p.m.," the guide said.

Lin picked a rifle and a pair of night goggles. They group scattered. They could monitor each other's position on the small tracker screens they wore on their wrists. Lin stayed with the minister.

The first sign of a target beeped on the walkie.

"I hit one," the British man said.

Lin and the minister changed course towards the direction.

"It's a flesh wound. He is coming your way fast."

The minister smiled, readying his crossbow. He lay flat in the grass.

"You shoot to wound."

"Why not just kill the animal?"

"Where is the fun in that? Of course, it will die eventually. We try to make it as long as we can."

"Has anyone died on these hunts? What happens if a person dies?"

"Nothing. We signed waivers," Nick said.

Moments later, the minister steadied his crossbow and shot. He shouted, "Bull's eye!"

Lin watched through the night goggles. She could see the blood under the night optics as the lion dragged its lame rear legs along.

The minister loaded another arrow and readied the weapon. He fired. This arrow thrust into the opposite thigh, sending the lion into the grass. It struggled to stand. Lin watched the minister load another arrow.

"Let me try," Lin said.

"Just don't kill him yet," the minister said.

The minister handed her the loaded weapon. Lin lay flat and aimed. She shot the arrow. The arrow struck the lion below the jawline. She watched as the lion fell. It twitched a few times, then lay still.

She heard the minister gasp.

"You killed him!"

"I'm so sorry. I didn't mean to."

"That's an excellent shot for a mistake."

"I wanted it to go longer, but, oh well, I guess the fun is over."

"You and I won the prize, so we get to keep the carcass."

The beacon signaled everyone back to the car where they toasted Nick's victory with scotch.

CHAPTER
THIRTY-ONE

REGGIE RECEIVED a call from Clive as they waited for an Uber to the Vic Falls airport. Her features tensed while she maintained a calm voice.

When she finished, Six said, "What was it?"

"It was Clive."

"What happened?"

Reggie looked around, then said, "The safari guide, Conwell, is dead. Body found by local fishermen," she said. "That's all I know for now."

"When?"

"This morning."

"Do you think it's because we talked to him?"

"I've been thinking the same."

"But what would this be for?"

"Sending a message. Someone might have seen us, and ratted him out," she said.

"Maybe. We don't know that yet."

"If the medical examiner results come back, then we know."

They instructed the Uber driver to take them to the regional hospital, where they waited in the lobby.

"This is my least favorite thing to do," Reggie said.

"Fortunately, my job doesn't require me to come back and check in my targets afterwards. I leave while they are still warm."

"Gross."

"Does it get better?"

"No. I guess you develop a shell for it. It's a job."

Joyce, the medical examiner, arrived. After exchanging pleasantries, as far as possible under the circumstances, they put on protective clothing and face masks, gloves, and booties. Joyce led them to the morgue. On a table was Joyce's half-finished lunch. This time the room was freezing.

Joyce pulled the Number 44 drawer out onto a large tray. She untied the strings around the plastic cover, then removed the straps on the plastic cover, revealing the large cut that bisected the man's body, from his chest down.

"I am only partway through the autopsy," she said.

The man's mouth was wide open, as if he had been laughing. Rigor mortis made his jaws stiff. Whatever his last breath was, it was clear he had had more to say when life had been snatched from him. Six and Reggie observed the body.

"Fortunately, the rain didn't wash away everything," Joyce said. "I found some skin scraps under his pinky nail. Looks like he gave a fight. I ran some DNA tests on it. I will send the results to you in a few hours. There is something I checked that doesn't add up," she added. "Our victim didn't drown. He was thrown in the river after he was already dead."

She wrenched the man's rigor mortised arm. Reggie and Six inched closer.

"You see these?" she said.

"Faint strap marks."

"Correct. Very faint now since the body was found late. I'm surprised the body survived the crocodiles. If they had found the body a few minutes later, all these marks would be gone. And as you can see, a chunk of his right thigh is missing. Impressed the wild animals didn't tear him up completely. I also did some blood tests. High levels of triple Z."

"So he was drugged?"

"Correct."

"That changes some things."

"Since the start of the power plant construction, all kinds of illegal substances have been flowing in here. Can't tell you how many I've seen in here from overdose. Used to all be young. Now older adults."

Six and Reggie were speechless.

"Oh, yes," said Joyce. "Go to the E.R. Kids barely reaching puberty, destroying themselves on these drugs, especially triple Z. But hey, money for the city."

"Doc, can I ask for a favor?" Six said.

"Would you run some DNA tests on these?" He held up a Ziplock bag of cigar butts. "I kept them in my fridge."

"Smart guy. Only if you promise a drink."

"I promise. After all this is done."

"Hm. Can't wait." She smiled. "And just call me Joyce."

She took the Ziplock bag from Six and scrutinized it. Six also handed her his card.

"I should have the sequencing results tomorrow."

Reggie and Six thanked Joyce and left.

"What was in that bag?"

"Some potential DNA lead. I don't know if it will pan out yet, but right now we need anything we can get."

"Why would they kill the guy?" Reggie said.

"Throwing us off our trail."

"But he was part of our trail?"

"Guess they are trying to waste our time. They know it will take weeks to find out what happened to him going through the proper channels."

"But we are not going through the proper bullshit channels of power. Let's go see where they found him. We might get some clues."

THIRTY-TWO

SIX'S PHONE BUZZED. It was Joyce. He put the phone on speaker so Reggie could hear.

"Hi, Joyce."

"Hey, Six," she said flirtatiously. Reggie rolled her eyes. "I got the DNA results from Clive's fingernail debris. Couldn't find a match for any person of interest."

"So that's a dead end?"

"Yes, but I also checked our library for samples we have run before."

"And?"

"A few months ago, I ran the same DNA results from a girl, another homicide, found at a dumpster downtown."

"Still no match?"

"I'm sorry, nothing more."

"Thanks, Joyce, for getting this done quickly."

"You're welcome. And wait, I did sequence the DNA from the cigar butts you sent me. It matched some of the victims I've worked on in the past."

"It did?"

"Yes."

"Thanks, Joyce. Can you text me the results? It's part of the investigation."

"If you say so. Right away. I'm doing this for the drink."

"I know. Thanks."

SIX AND REGGIE stopped by the safari guide's house on their way to the crime scene.

At the guide's house, Six consoled the wife. The woman's eyes were red and puffy, evidently from crying and sleep deprivation. After sharing their condolences and promising the woman they would do everything in their power to catch the person who did this, Reggie asked the questions.

"When last did you see your husband?"

"Yesterday morning."

"Did he say anything?"

"No," she said. "Same routine. Ate breakfast, took the kids to school in the Jeep."

"Anything unusual in the way he acted?"

"He was excited a bit. I wanted to ask him. But I was just glad he had only a few hours to work today. He even promised to go watch our son's soccer game."

"Anything suspicious that you saw?" Reggie said.

The wife sobbed. "After the incident, he was having nightmares. He was always afraid someone would kill him."

"Did he say who?"

"He never told me anything. The man seemed unnerved, like he had changed after the event. I suspected it was work."

"Did he ever go to the river at night?"

"No, not on weekdays."

"One more thing," Reggie said, holding her hand. "Did your husband drink or use any drugs?"

"My husband would never do that."

"Are you sure?"

"He was one of the people teaching the kids at the local high school to stay away from those substances. He would never. He was a good Christian man. And loved his family and took pride in his job as a safari guide. He would not risk the lives of his visitors by using drugs. That man had good character and values."

They all nodded.

Reggie handed the woman a printed list of contacts and asked her to phone if she thought of anything else.

"We will do our best to find whoever did this," Six said.

The woman nodded, but her features were resigned.

"In the meantime, I'll have one of our officers keep an eye on you, just in case. I'll be checking on you every day. Phone me if you need anything."

"Thank you," said the wife, although she did not have a phone.

The drive to the crime scene was quiet as both Six and Reggie contemplated what had just happened.

"Do you think he didn't tell us something?" Reggie finally broke the silence.

"I'm starting to think the same."

"But why would he lie?"

"He has a family that he loves. That's one thing that can make a man do the unthinkable."

"Why would someone kill him?"

"If someone killed him," Six corrected her.

"But the wife said he was standing up against drug use at the high school. Maybe he stepped on the wrong toes."

"That's possible."

"Makes sense that they would pump him with the same drugs he was fighting against."

"We'll nail these bastards!" said Reggie, and punched the steering wheel.

Six and Reggie saw nothing new at the crime scene and spent most of the day at the station going over reports. The postmortem results didn't line up.

"From where the body was found, he could have been killed anywhere upstream."

"Joyce said he was thrown into the river after he was already dead."

THIRTY-FOUR

THE DEATH OF CONWELL, the safari guide, had given Six more motivation for Six to nail the bastards who did this—for the guide's wife and kids. Though rarely affected by events, Six decided instead of having a drink at the Club to walk two kilometers to a Chinatown bar. It would clear his mind and maybe ease his sense of guilt, and so far Chinatown had been just a name.

Six waited until it was dark to walk to the settlement. He proceeded on foot past hundreds of makeshift identical white mobile homes, all alike. These housed the migrant Chinese workers and other foreign workers brought in to work at the fourth colliery and hydro-power station.

He gave way to a line of cars, then crossed an intersection into an alley leading to a central point with shops and kiosks. He passed through lines of hostels and prefab cottages which housed migrant workers at Hwange Colliery, workers paid peanuts, to the pub where loud music was playing. He opened its door on the smells of smoke, human stench, sweat, urine and alcohol.

The sign above the front read "Liu's Happy Corner".

Of course it could have been just a common name in Chinatown. But Six remembered what Clive had said: that Liu not only owned China-town but ruled it.

Loud music, noise, cigarette smoke, and filth. Six paused to adjust his vision and breathing. He squeezed his way to the bar counter. A white guy in blue coveralls lined with reflectors on both the arms and pant legs was disrespectful to Six. "Don't mind him," someone said, tapping Six on the shoulder. "He's just miserable. You know what they say, hurting people hurt people."

Six turned. This man ordered a beer for Six, who declined. Six summoned the bartender.

"Get a beer for my friend here," Six said. "Water for me."

"Thanks, mate," the man said, exposing his orange-stained teeth, with the two top front teeth missing. "What about you? You don't drink?"

"I do. Just not today."

Six did not enjoy drinking, though he did occasionally. He functioned better that way. He always wanted to remember his steps, remember what he did or said yesterday. Alcohol tended to make people do stupid things they would regret. Like throwing one's life away. His mind drifted to the memory of the night a drunk driver had killed his parents. To make matters worse, the drunk driver, a promising young college athlete, had survived unscathed. He suppressed the memory.

"Then what is a guy like you doing here?"

"Looking for someone."

"Who? Maybe I know him?"

"Liu. The man in charge of the colliery."

The man leaned in, his breath full of alcohol and smoke. "I wouldn't say that name again if I were you."

"Why not?"

"He's like a god around here. You don't want to mess with him. Let's say nothing good happens to the very few people who deliberately cross his path. He has ears everywhere. Wrong word, you disappear. Best advice for you is to zip your mouth and trudge along."

Six looked around the bar.

"Who are you, anyway?"

Six slid his investigator's badge onto the table.

"Oh," the man said. He did not bother checking the badge.

"So, tell me, where does he live?"

"Everyone knows his house. It's the biggest mansion in this shithole. He does all the dirty work for the mayor."

"Tell me more."

"Yeah. That son of a bitch. He doesn't want his hands dirty, so he hires Liu and his goons to do the job. Liu is his right-hand man. That's why all the employees never strike. You raise a grievance today, next morning we hear you had an accident at work, or you disappear."

"I heard he doesn't stay here often."

"He doesn't. Who would? This place is an oven during the summer. Only us peasants bake here because we don't have a choice. If I had money like him, I'd go somewhere."

"Interesting."

"But you are in luck. The boss is in town today."

"How do you know?"

"Who else drives three black Land Cruisers? It's him and his entourage."

Six ordered the man another can of beer.

"Do you know why he is here early?"

"I heard people at work saying it has to do with the hydro-power station. Something happening this weekend. Just saying, mate, and forget I said it."

"You know where the house is?"

"Go out, turn right two blocks, then left. You will see a bigger house there with a fence and hounds. That's Liu's palace."

Six slapped a five-dollar bill on the counter and said good night.

The man smiled. "Go right on, mate. To your own death!"

THIRTY-FIVE

LIU'S COMPOUND WAS FENCED, perched on slightly elevated bare ground. The structures were still so brand-new that there was no garden or greenery.

The moon was high up, partly swiftly being covered by dark clouds. Then came some thunder. A summer storm. With gloves on, Six chose the wooden club from his bag and strapped the pistol to his belt just in case, although he hoped he wouldn't have to use it.

Six assessed the house. There were two men stationed at the front, and he guessed two more at the back. He waited, looking for hounds. There was no movement. From around the block Six flung a stone over the fence that landed a few feet away from the men guarding the back door.

One guard motioned the other to find the source of the noise. The moon was now completely covered, and it started raining, which camouflaged Six's black attire. He climbed over the fence, carefully fitting his feet between the barbs on top. He landed softly on the other side.

The other guard was still looking in the direction his partner had gone, speaking something into his radio. Before he could turn, Six jabbed him on the carotid, immediately paralyzing the man. He pulled the body to the side and waited in the shadow. His partner trotted back briskly, saying, "I think it was an animal—"

Six cut him off with an elbow to the throat before the man could finish, which knocked him out.

A bullet cracked, grazing the right side of Six's jacket. The rain and thunderstorm overshadowed the sound of the gun. He hadn't seen that guy. Then he saw two. He had never prayed, but he felt someone was watching over him—his parents, or God. That's why he was still alive. He was being saved for a bigger purpose.

Even startled and in shock, one of them men reached automatically for his gun. Six hit the man's hand with the wooden club and crushed his arm. Six followed that with a swift uppercut that muted any sound the man was about to make. He brought down the club onto the other man's skull. He crumpled to the ground.

Six checked their pulses and pulled the bodies to the side. He tiptoed into the house. He looked around for alarms and cameras, but only one room was lit, and he passed through the back hallway in darkness. The bright light came from one room at the end of the hall, and a voice was talking. A hound in a crate in the hallway looked at Six and growled. Then thunder struck, and the dog curled back into the corner of the crate, whining. *Poor thing, scared of the thunder,* Six thought. He passed it, tiptoeing, and backed into the shadows of a room that was like an office. The man talking paused.

"Anyone there?" the man's voice said.

Six froze.

"I'll call you right back. I think my dog got out of the cage again."

Then Six heard footsteps coming. Six waited. *Only one person.*

Six drove the wooden club into the man's midsection, stunning him, then slammed him forcefully toward the office desk. He flipped over the desk, reached for the drawer, but Six threw the club, which crashed into the man's wrist. Six then heaved across the room a cupboard filled with books, bottled scotch, and glassware. Liu did his best to throw everything in his sight at Six. A wine glass caught Six on the chin. Six smashed the man's face with several punches that fractured his nose and several bones on his face, leaving it flattened, bloody and mucus-soaked.

"That's for Louis and Conwell!"

Liu slumped to the floor. "You're too late," the man said, spitting blood. "We are going to make a killing."

"You've two choices. Either you tell me what I want, or I'll kill you."

"Killing me won't help you. We know who you are. They will know you did this."

"It'll give me satisfaction."

"We will kill you and your officer girlfriend. And when we are done with you, you will wish you never set foot here."

Shit! They'll hurt Reggie!

"I think my men are already having fun with her right now. You're too late."

Six planted a blade into Liu's thigh. The man winced. Then he laughed again, hysterically.

"I'm just a small fish in the pond. You kill me, more will come."

Six ignored him and rummaged through the desk drawers, taking photos.

"You are dead meat. You are fucking dead, man!" Liu said.

"I will be waiting."

"They'll kill you and everyone you've ever loved."

Six planted an elbow blow to the Liu's temple. Then Six checked his pulse. The man was dead. Six loaded all the papers from the drawer into his backpack. In the lighted room Six laid his cellphone atop Liu's phone. Now he had it all. He tapped open some folders and learned what he needed to know.

He texted both Lin and Reggie and pinned the rendezvous address, at the new colliery. He wrote *Hurry*, but it would take all of them half an hour.

THIRTY-SIX

REGGIE AND LIN arrived a few seconds apart.

Six was waiting near to the storage facilities in the shadows.

"Who's she?" asked Reggie, motioning to Lin.

"Lin. A friend. MI6. She's with us."

Reggie opened her mouth to protest.

"You'll acquaint later. We don't have enough time until someone finds out and alerts the others. I know where Liu's girls are and we will get them out of here. Follow me," Six said.

"Liu will have us killed."

"Dead," Six said.

"I didn't mean for you to kill him," Reggie said.

"That was the only way to get the answers."

"We still have to follow the law."

"He left me no choice. The choice was I die, or he dies. I chose the latter," Six said. "Lin has been working on the missing girls and sex trafficking case here. And I just found where they are."

Lin was about to speak when Six motioned them to be quiet. It began to rain and thunder in earnest, the earth turning to mud.

The three waited and listened. Then Six signaled, and they crept in single file towards the first shed, a boxcar minus wheels.

Four men with AK-47s patrolled the front of this shed.

"We should call backup," Reggie said into Six's ear.

"No," Six said. "It has to be done quietly. We don't want a bloodbath. We can take out these guys."

While they were still talking, all four men tumbled to the ground and lay flat.

"What just happened?"

"It was Lin," said Six. "Dammit. She's stubborn. Wants to have all the fun."

Lin flashed her small flashlight two times. Reggie and Six, dripping wet, hunched and scrambled to the entrance.

Six flashed his light into the shed. Dozens of kids looked back at them, squeezing away from the door.

"Come on, guys, out. Move."

"Police," Reggie said, flashing her badge. "We won't hurt you. Let's go."

Six led them several hundred yards outside the perimeter, where a school bus waited on an incline, lights dimmed.

"Everyone, quiet. Quickly."

Six was the last to board the bus and

scanned the area to see if anyone had seen them, then said to the driver, "We're good. Let's go!"

The bus rolled through mud for about twenty meters, then merged into the main road. And the driver turned on the engine.

One grimy little girl shouldered her way forward through the aisle and hugged Lin. The girl cried. "You're safe now," Lin said. "Did they hurt you?"

The girl shook her head.

"You know her?" Reggie said to Lin.

"Yes. I came here in the same container."

Reggie stared at her.

"It's part of the job."

The bus driver knew his way around. After crossing the Victoria Falls bridge, he switched on the full headlights and they sped into Zambia. Lin spent the next few minutes communicating with her contacts at the British military base in Zambia.

While the bus roared through the rainstorm, Six moved up behind the driver and asked his name.

"I am Conwell Jr," the driver said.

An hour later, they reached the base. The kids filed into large halls with bunk beds. Lin hugged the girl again, and several others.

"Here, keep this on." She slid the girl a bracelet the kid had once given to her. "It will keep you safe."

The girl clung to her.

"Let's leave while it's still raining," Lin said. "Dawn will be coming soon."

CHAPTER
THIRTY-SEVEN

THE THREE MEN sat facing the large mahogany table. Opposite, mayor Gideon Hove sat in what had been Liu's chair, looking outside, cigar in hand. He swiveled his chair around to face them.

The men trembled.

"Can someone explain to me how one of my best men died and thirty-seven kids disappeared without a trace?"

They glanced at each other, numb. They knew any wrong word could mean death in cold blood. The boss, as they called him, was known for his erratic behavior and temper. Finally, the taller one in the middle said, "It was an ambush, sir. We did not see it coming."

"How many men attacked you?"

The man licked his dry lips. "I only saw one."

"One man overcame three of you single-handedly?" The mayor glared at them.

"Sir, this man was—" he paused, choosing

his words carefully, "actually, there were two. This woman was fast."

"Woman?"

"She separated us from our weapons, and then a big man with a club came."

"Did you see their faces? What does this boogeyman look like?"

"A big man, sir. But his face was covered, and we couldn't see in the dark."

"And none of your crew heard them or the commotion?"

"We were the only ones on patrol, sir, and it was thundering and raining. We had been alerted about another threat."

"Was the threat real?"

"Turned out to be a false alarm. We were ambushed less than a minute after our return."

"She was smooth as a cat," the man on the left said. "Well trained."

"He had a wooden club," the man on his right said. "The only thing I remember was a thud on my temple."

"A wooden club?"

"Yes, sir."

The mayor rose from the table and sat at the front, now staring the men in the face.

"How does a woman and a baseball-bat-wielding man disarm my best guards with AK-47s?"

"Sir, this happened fast."

"Is that why I pay you?"

"Sir, please. We have an insider investigating."

The mayor nodded to one of the guards circling the room around the three men. The man brought a silver case. The man retrieved a pistol, released the safety, and corked it.

"No one heard the kids leaving; forty people, leaving. No one!"

The room fell silent.

"Do you know how much money that will set me back?"

He planted the gun's nose on the taller man. In all fairness, if the power dynamics were reversed or equal, the man could easily crush the mayor. But in this case, he was powerless. The mayor seemed to enjoy making the big man tremble in fear.

"A lot, sir," the man said. "It won't happen again—"

Before he could finish his sentence, a bullet went through his jaw out the back of his head, carrying with it brain tissue and all.

The other two men trembled, looking around them. The rest of their crew flashed their weapons in case the men decided to run for it.

"You failed, and I can't have that. I can't have incompetent people around me."

"Sir! We have families."

"They will be better off without you. You're a waste to society."

In a split second, the mayor planted a bullet in each forehead and the men collapsed to the ground, blood spraying across the wooden floor. "Clean this up," the mayor told his crew.

The mayor's cellphone rang. He wiped

droplets of blood off his shirt with a handker-chief before he answered.

After hearing a rush of angry words from the other end, the mayor said, "I'm sorry, sir. We've had a minor setback. It's nothing that can't be fixed."

"If these hiccups continue to happen, that will derail the bidding meeting. And we can't have that!" the man barked from the other end of the line.

"We're taking care of it."

"Don't disappoint me."

The mayor paused. "Sir, shouldn't we figure out what's happening?" the mayor said. "We don't want to lose any more people."

"Speed, my friend, is the key. The earliest bird catches the fattest worm. If I stop, whoever is doing this will think I'm weak. Kings don't stop. We advance, no matter the casualties. I can't halt the work; the board is depending on me. I need this done."

"I will take care of it."

The mayor hung up and wiped sweat from his brow. He said to an aide, "Bring that insider from the P.D. I want to have a chat with him."

"Yes, sir."

THE MAYOR then phoned one of Liu's deputies to learn more about the missing chil-dren. "Our clients will be mad. We will lose clients over this. This year we wanted to do something special for them," the mayor said.

"We will find whoever did this. We have people in the police."

"We can't keep losing money. I invested a lot in this."

"We are sure these people used only one vehicle. It wouldn't be difficult to spot forty children in one vehicle. But there were no tracks and none of the roadblocks saw them."

"Idiots. Use whichever means you can to find if anyone heard or saw something. Whatever it takes. It's a small town."

"Yes, Mayor."

"I need answers by tomorrow. The big event is on Saturday."

"Yes, sir."

"Get me the police chief on the line."

CHAPTER
THIRTY-EIGHT

SIX AND REGGIE met at their favorite coffee shop. Once settled, Reggie said, "That was brave of you, rescuing the kids."

"Teamwork. If you and Lin didn't show up, I don't think I'd have been able to pull it off."

"How did you know?"

"About the kids? Lin told me yesterday. Then I did some research. I also knew there was one place I could get that information."

"From Liu."

"Yes."

"I'm just happy all those kids are safe."

"Me too," Six said. "I'm surprised Liu had less manpower than I thought. He didn't have a personal bodyguard. I'd guess a place like that would be teeming with armed guards. The dog was caged, and there wasn't even a kitchen maid."

They talked about other things. Then Six said, "We are getting close to nailing the head of the snake. Several of the documents I got from Liu might prove useful."

"Are you sending those to me?"

"I think you should stay away from the Liu case for now."

"Why?"

"You have six disappeared and two murders to look into. And there is a mole at the station. Keep the kids' rescue between you, me, and Lin."

"You think someone is leaking the investigation out?"

"Could be any of the officers or your partner. I have always had a hunch he can't be trusted. I know for sure we have a mole at the station," Six said, "and it can be no one else."

"I don't think he would sell us out or go that far. In the past he has done good work."

"Sometimes hunches are wrong."

"Why would he waste his career on this?"

"My M.O. is I don't rationalize people's bull-shit. I try to believe them the first time they show me who they are. Better sooner than later."

"Should we confront him?"

"There is no way in hell he's going to admit to anything unless we have evidence. But we have nothing but suspicions," Six said.

"You might be overreaching here," Reggie said.

CHAPTER
THIRTY-NINE

SIX'S PHONE BUZZED. Six lifted it to his ear and then banged it down on the desk.

"The bastard!"

"What? What happened?" said Reggie.

"You remember the DNA I had Joyce run from cigar stubs. It matched the DNA found from several girls Joyce had examined previously."

"Meaning the minister is involved?"

"Yes."

"I forwarded the results to my contact at HQ and just had matching DNA results from a wanted war criminal from Mozambique—the guy who terrorized Mozambique in the '80s and '90s."

"Who? Matsanga?"

Six looked impressed. "Girl, you know your history. He is now Zimbabwe's minister of infrastructure development."

"What?"

"They have identified him. Just got the intel

in from my source. It was through a coincidental hacking into a DNA ancestral database, which matched what their organization had."

"So, the minister wanted to know his heritage?"

"Maybe to justify his ethnic cleansing."

"Where did you get the initial comparison?"

"From a local Mozambican doctor who operated on some of his female victims from the late '80s! Everyone seems to have forgotten about him. Everyone thinks he died decades ago. DNA testing was not a thing back then. He is probably getting too comfortable as well."

"But could that be his son, uncle?"

"That's too much of a stretch. The DNA sequence is never a hundred percent similar. Plus, I also took images of him that were analyzed for age, and several facial features that do not change even after plastic surgery, which the guy seemed to have done minimal. I mean, no one would suspect that a wanted mass murderer is holding a cabinet position in another country."

"Truth always comes out. What do we do now?"

"We dig more, now that we have a target. My boss once told us to catch the head of the snake—you may be surprised that all these guys are all sponsored by same people, companies, or countries."

"That's going to take a while."

"I know. I'd prefer to put a bullet between his eyes."

"How're you getting all that info?"

"I used some unconventional ways."

She glared at him. "Just be careful."

"These guys have friends in high places. Our intel that we've gathered for many years shows the Portuguese were involved. Same system, now just shifted to China in charge," Six said. "At least the Chinese don't hide behind a facade of missionary work, spreading the word of God, or sending peace-keeping troops. The Chinese give loans and high interest rates or ridiculous clauses. They even built the African Union headquarters, and right here in Zimbabwe they are building the parliament building. They bring their own people to do the job, not locals. Mostly for espionage. We let them build the African Union parliament. The most important building in Africa."

"For now, let's focus on the Vic Falls case. We have a trip to South Africa tomorrow, remember?"

"I know."

"We will need a mountain of evidence to nail him down, and it has to be done swiftly before he disappears."

"We're getting close," Six said.

CHAPTER
FORTY

THE PAIR LANDED at the Johannesburg's O.R. Tambo International Airport just past noon. They bought two train passes at the vending machine and boarded the Gautrain to the University of the Witwatersrand. The bullet train sped past the FNB Stadium on the right, one marvel from the 2010 FIFA World Cup. The outside of the stadium was graffiti-ridden, showing signs of dilapidation, as was often the fate of these multimillion-dollar megastructures after the event was over. They got off at Park Station and walked the remaining few blocks to the university campus. The weather was delightful, with a gentle breeze.

They asked a group of students leaving the cafeteria where to find Professor de Klerk. The students giggled and gestured at an old man sauntering to the administration offices with a cane, slightly bent forward. Six and Reggie caught up with him.

"Professor de Klerk!" Reggie said.

The old man turned slowly, making sure the salad bowl he was carrying did not fall to the ground.

"Hello," he said. "Sorry, my memory isn't as sharp. Do I know you? Are you in one of my classes?"

His eyes moved from Reggie up to Six.

"No, professor. We're a little too old for university."

"Then?"

"We would like to talk to you about something," Six said.

"That sounds insidious from the way you said it. What can I help you with?"

"We want to ask you a few questions about your work."

"African mythic literature," Reggie said.

The man's features loosened. "I'm all ears. Humor me. Anything in particular?"

"Your work in the Zambezi region."

"How do I know you're not amateurs just having fun at it? Like many others before, who made me believe I was insane."

"Sir, we assure you. Anything you can give us is valuable."

"Why is this important to you?"

"We are just curious," Six said.

The professor looked up at Six skeptically. "You are not students. But you're interested in my scholarship. Something doesn't add up." He turned to walk away.

"There are six children missing at Victoria

Falls," Reggie said. "My partner and I think it's connected."

"I have been following that story. Are you cops?"

"We are private investigators."

"And you think something else captured these children?"

"Yes."

"Could be crocodiles. The Zambezi river is infested with hundreds of those filthy creatures."

"Searchers have found no remains in all crocodiles captured within the vicinity. If it were true, at least one of them would have remains in it."

"Something like this has happened before. Come with me. I want to show you something," de Klerk said, and led them into the administration building through two massive wooden front doors.

The narrow corridor had walls decorated with portraits of famous alumni from the university and several donors. His office was room 114, with his name etched on the left side of the door frame. Six held the salad bowl while the professor sorted through a bunch of keys from his pocket, finally settling on a silver one.

The office was dark, with a sliver of light through the small window, most of it blocked by boxes. De Klerk switched the lights on. Depictions of mermaids, primates, Bigfoot, and witches on hyenas and flying in winnowing baskets and on brooms covered on entire wall. A leather rocking chair was in the corner, under a yellow lamp. Everything was untidy: artifacts, bones, preserved insects in airtight jars. Books and papers were strewn everywhere. "Sit," he said, pointing at two folding metal chairs.

Reggie and Six sat. They watched the professor rampage through piles of papers on his shelf without saying a word. He then pulled a faded green folder. He flung through the pages before dumping the folder on another pile of books.

"It's been a long time ago since I worked on this: way back during the building of the Kariba Dam. It collapsed, killing hundreds. These are handwritten accounts from local people. And of course, science didn't pay attention to any warnings. They still carried on, building. The locals said they could see what happened."

Reggie and Six waited.

"Oh, hold on, there is something else."

Six and Reggie watched the professor comb through another pile of notebooks on the wooden shelf. He pulled one and blew the dust from its binding.

"Several of the locals I talked to described something like what you're saying. Some of those claims." He pointed with his finger to a section scribbled.

"Professor, what's the likelihood of the kids and this being connected?"

"As I said, it is not the first time something like this has happened. Were you taught about what happened in the '60s? Eighty-six men died constructing the bridge, some of them Italian prisoners. And no one knew why. Some blamed the engineers. Others said it was forces of nature."

"But how did they solve it?"

"They solved that by going to the local elders, *sangoma*, traditional healers. Only then were they able to resume construction."

"Are you saying there had to be a blood sacrifice?"

"Maybe or maybe not. But I know there are forces in nature that have to be respected. To build a dam is to restrain a force of nature."

"Is that what's happening now?"

"There is a pattern." He pointed to the different articles. "Ever since the president opened the country to foreign investment to build the first hydro-power plant, many people have been disappearing."

"I remember reading about that," Reggie said.

"I believe construction of that first hydro-power plant spawned other events, the mysterious disappearances, and earthquakes," the professor said. "December third, two employees disappeared and were never found. Three tourists met same disastrous accidents. Stories of visitors mysteriously disappearing after construction begun. Who knows how many locals have disappeared? Most of the workers are undocumented, so no one cares.

"Same event happened in 1960 during the construction of Kariba dam. The mayor consulted the necromancer. Locals call them *san-*

goma. That area around the falls is viewed by natives as sacrosanct," de Klerk said. "You don't remember, but there were debates on TV about how this will force displacement of hundreds of people, just like the earlier project did to the Tonga people in the 1950s. The whole battle threatened to halt construction. The elders warned against it."

"But the government would not discuss that openly."

"Money rules. More money, and the project carried on. The Rhodesian government tried the same in the 1960s, when the Kariba dam was destroyed. Keeping it under wraps since then. They were only able to rebuild the Kariba dam after consulting local elders and local religious leaders and the necromancer."

The professor continued. "The massive earthquake last year. Nothing like this before. That's no coincidence. I know experts explained it away with climate change as the cause."

"Professor, are you trying to tell us that all the earthquakes and missing people are connected?"

"Yes."

"But how do you explain all the—?"

"There are forces far greater than ours at play here."

Reggie said, "Professor, in some of your African mythic literature studies, you mention a connection to the dragon belief in East Asian cultures. The embodiment of immortality, power, and prosperity. Is this something plausible?"

Professor de Klerk pondered the question.

"I wouldn't disagree," he said. He flipped through the notebook to a page titled in blue ink: *Tales of a giant monster that roared in the falls.* Reggie and Six looked on.

"*Nyaminyami?*" Reggie said.

"That's one name the locals called it. All Tonga people along the Zambezi worshipped and offered blood sacrifices to the *Nyaminyami*. Usually livestock, eland, and other animals." He turned to the next page and showed several sketches. "These are representations of some of the structures the people built as the *Nyaminyami* for worship. I got these from talking to traditional leaders."

Six scrutinized the sketches. "Is it possible to visit these? They seem to be all different," Six said.

"Correct. My understanding is none of the inhabitants ever saw the creature. In fact, they believed seeing one was a misfortune, and anyone who saw it disappeared. Only selected religious leaders approached designated sacrificial sites. The most sacred was Victoria Falls, of course. Ideas of what the *Nyaminyami* looks like ranged from a giant snake, a monstrous slug, a lizard with wings, or even a crocodile possibly. No one knows."

"Where at Victoria Falls?"

"It is park land now, a wilderness conservation area. I was last there in the early '80s. It must have reverted to jungle by now."

"There is a lot of conservation area there."

"Approximately here," said the professor, and made a sketch with his pen.

"You're not the first ones to show interest in this recently," he said.

"Did anyone else ask you?"

"The only other person who was interested in some of my work was Mr. Hellstrom. I'd say about a year ago."

"Hellstrom? The Dutch art collector."

"You know him?"

"He has sponsored a lot of museums across the globe, even donated some famous pieces to the Louvre and D.C. Museum of Natural History."

"Oh yes. He is a good guy," the professor said. "He has been a benefactor for our university for years. Everyone knows him here."

"When did you last talk to him?"

"A couple of months back. He said his legacy now was to preserve African artifacts. That's why he was interested in my work."

"What else?"

"He asked questions. We chatted about artifacts, relics, and all. Quite interesting fellow."

"Did he take anything?"

"He just thanked me and left. Donated two million dollars to the university a few days later."

Reggie and Six exchanged glances.

"Thank you, Professor."

"Hope I answered your questions."

"You did. Can we contact you if we have questions?"

"I'm always ready to talk about science." He handed Reggie a business card.

"Thank you so much."

They rose and exited the office. As they walked out the building towards the car, Reggie was googling "sangoma Johannesburg" on her cellphone.

"There is one about thirty miles from here," Reggie said.

ALTHOUGH SIX HAD BEEN SKEPTICAL, Reggie had convinced Six to go with her to consult the *sangoma*. They paid and were asked to wait. They sat on tree stumps outside a hut, told the *sangoma* was dealing with another person.

"Do you think this is worth it?"

"Nothing to lose. These guys know a lot. All the oral tradition is passed down in the family. Just didn't have books."

A couple emerged from the hut. Moments later, a man came outside and informed them the healer was ready.

"That's her husband," Reggie whispered. "Just do what I do. Get that American look off your face."

Reggie clapped her hands before entering the hut, at the same time addressing the healer, and respectfully requested permission to enter. Six clapped once and didn't say a word. The woman inside said they could enter.

The healer was dressed in traditional Zulu costume, with huge bracelets of brown beads on her hands and ankles, and a large necklace across her chest, and a feather headband. She sat with her legs crisscrossed.

The hut was dark, except for the light from a single candle in the corner. In the candlelight, Six, seated uncomfortably cross-legged on the floor, could see jelly jars of herbs, leaves, stones, bones, twigs, soil, teeth, and fur. Without saying another word, the woman opened two jars, and retrieved a tusk, a hippo tooth, fur, and some bones. She chanted, shaking the relics in her hands, then threw them to the floor, where they scattered. Six moved his leg as a bone fell close to him. She continued chanting.

After several chants and gibberish songs, the *sangoma* studied the relics, moving from one item to the next, then back again. Six glanced at Reggie. She was intently observing the woman.

The woman lifted her gaze to Six and Reggie. "My children of the law. I see you are troubled about why people are disappearing at the falls." She paused. "Ancestors lament with you. Big business and greed is destroying their sanctuaries. They have chosen you, my children."

Six shifted in his seat, while maintaining his focus on the woman.

The woman then said in a deep, unsettling voice, "They shall perish! They must be stopped! You should stop them!"

Reggie and Six sat there, stunned.

"But be careful, my children. Some things

prefer not to be disturbed. You already have a way to go. Use that, and it shall direct you."

Six and Reggie exchanged a glance.

After a few moments, the woman's frantic movements stopped, and she spoke in a normal voice. "You can go now. You already have a way."

She gave them incense that she instructed them to burn and charms to chant before entering the forest. Six begrudgingly and silently accepted these. Reggie thanked her. The husband led them out, where several other people were waiting to come in.

CHAPTER
FORTY-TWO

"I WISH she had been more specific," said Reggie.

Six held the map while Reggie drove. They were following the route sketched on the map from Professor de Klerk towards a spot he had marked "Kariba caves."

"How far are we?" Reggie said.

"Twenty minutes," Six said.

"Do you think we are wasting time?"

"I liked scavenger hunts as a kid. This might turn out to be a cool adventure."

They laughed.

"It's pretty straightforward. We should be able to find it quickly."

"I hope so. I'm sure trees have clogged the way now."

"Let's hope not."

They drove in silence for a while.

"Take the next right turn," Six said.

Reggie steered the car off the main road onto a gravel strip. Six hopped out and unlocked the metal gate above a grid designed to keep animals out. They drove along the bumpy road for several minutes in silence.

"Next right," Six said.

They reached a dead end with massive trees and undergrowth. They could see the Falls from one side.

"I guess it's on foot now."

After putting on bug spray, Six put on his waterproof jacket and chose the wooden club and a pistol as weapons, locking the pistol into his thigh strap. Reggie put on her waterproof jacket as well. She chose a Beretta and strapped it to her waist holster. They carried their backpacks. The showers from the falls turned the adjacent forest into a perennial rain forest. The wind whispered across the evergreens.

The forest teemed with screeches, screams, and whistles from birds and other forest life. Because this was a national park, Six and Reggie were nervous about lions and other wild animals. The place was known for venomous black mambas as well.

"Now I know why they call it Mosi-oa-Tunya," Six said. "Can't even see where I'm going. Thankful for the compass."

After a minute, "It's here!" Reggie said. "The black mamba. I can smell it."

"How do you know?"

"My mom could tell by the smell. They release a distinct, unpleasant smell."

"Is it true that they only bite on the top of heads? I heard they can stand on the tip of their tail."

"Quiet. Watch your step."

Rainbows hung in the mist as they navigated the gorge into its deepest parts. They trudged on the damp mulch for several minutes until they reached a small clearing. There was a massive boulder on one side. Six and Reggie walked around it until they found a small opening. Six led the way in.

In the pitch-black cave they used flashlights. It was cold in there despite the scorching heat outside. The small crevice opened into a large clearing.

"Do you see this?" Reggie said, pointing her flashlight to the cave ceiling. Six looked up.

The entirety of the cave ceiling was painted with colorful preserved murals on the wall depicting how the San people lived. Spears, short-legged people, half-animal, half-human creatures, wild animals, and something that looked like a hunting party and a group of humans out gathering food. Part of it was weathered away. It was like a colorful clay mosaic in the cave wall.

"This is insane!"

Reggie moved her light to one wall. "This looks like a religious ceremony."

Six looked over. "How do you know?"

"It looks similar to drawings found in other Khoisan dwellings." The mural showed something like a sacrificial offering of a bull. Drops of blood, fire, and a religious procession on one side, with dancers and spectators.

"The snake-slug, sun, elands, and impalas represent symbolic religious meanings. These signs mean the snake creature gave life," Reggie said. "Pretty much the same for most of the Bantu people. Our earliest ancestors."

A smaller wall scene depicted eland being driven into tunnels with people wearing horrified faces.

"Is that what I think it is?"

Reggie studied the mural.

"Big fire and cattle dripping blood. Sacrifices. Possible religious procession."

"What about that?" Six said, pointing at another small mural which portrayed a group of humans in a trance below zigzagged lines resembling lightning bolts. Their faces evidently in agony.

"You think they did human sacrifice?"

Eerie silence followed. They reached a dead end. The waterfall was much louder.

"Why do I feel like we are right next to the falls?" Reggie said.

"Because we are."

"But there's no way through."

"Maybe there's a tunnel somewhere."

They searched. There was no further opening. They took pictures and left.

"No one has discovered this?" said Six.

"Obviously, because the professor had never heard of it. I say we leave it as is," Reggie said, scraping mud from her shoes. "Otherwise the world will descend on this place. Don't want it to end up being a tourist wasteland."

As they drove back on the gravel road, they passed a herd of elephants. Reggie slowed down. Suddenly, one elephant charged towards them. Reggie switched the gear into reverse, swerved, just missing a tree, then turned the Jeep around in the opposite direction through bumpy grass and mud. The elephant gave up the chase. Six and Reggie watched in the mirror as the giant mammal faded into a speck.

"She is the queen of the jungle!" Six said.

"That was a close one."

FORTY-THREE

AS SOON AS he entered his clubroom and removed his muddy boots, Six quickly checked several things he had set in place to see if anyone had tampered with them. The Do Not Disturb sign was still hanging outside his door, so he did not expect that housekeeping had cleaned his suite. His shorts were neatly folded on the shelf, t-shirts still in the same location. The bed looked neat, sheets unmoved, the way he had left them. He looked around, searching for more. Then he noticed the bible had moved. He always left it on the side of the nightstand, aligned with the edge. Now it was slightly moved up, just a few millimeters.

On the other side of town, Reggie parked the Jeep on the sidewalk. She liked to go through the rear door of her bed-and-breakfast. That way she did not bother her hosts. The metal gate had been propped open. She was about to remove her gun belt when her phone rang. It was Six.

"Thank God. Where are you?"

"Just parked my car. At home."

"You need to leave your place. Someone is after us. Be careful. My room was searched. I set my stuff in a way that only I can know when someone has been in."

"You sure it's not housekeeping?"

"I checked with them, and they said no one cleaned the suite. They have an electronic record of when the staff is in the rooms."

"But where would I go?"

"Come crash at my hotel room for a few days. It's dangerous not to."

Reggie heard glass breaking.

"Hold on," she told Six. "I heard something."

"What is it?"

"Hold on," she whispered. "Someone is here."

"Wait for me. I'm on my way."

Two bullets whizzed by, one catching Reggie's blouse and chipping the bark off a nearby avocado tree. She yelped. The bullet ricocheted off the stone wall.

"Shit!" She dove behind the tree onto the lawn. She waited a few seconds and then charged towards the door, her Beretta aimed.

She kicked the door open. Empty. The usually locked door that connected her room to the common hallway had been broken down and was open. The bathroom was empty. She charged into the hallway, into the main living room. The TV was smashed, and all furniture turned upside down. Her heart sank. She hoped the perpetrator had not killed the host family. Moments later, she heard an engine start. Rushing to the front, she saw a black minivan screeching away.

Twenty minutes later the driveway was lined with several police cars and an ambulance. They combed the house and bagged any potential evidence. Reggie sat on an ambulance bed while a medic tended to her shoulder wound where the bullet had grazed her. Shortly after, two concerned officers from the station joined her, asked a few questions, and recorded her statement.

Reggie found out the hosts had left for a different city for the holidays. She called them to tell them all was well and to stay away as long as they wanted.

Six arrived and saw a streak of blood on her blouse.

"How're you feeling?"

"It's just a flesh wound. Nothing painkillers can't help with."

They laughed.

"I'm just glad you're okay."

"Thanks, Six."

"Now they are showing muscle."

"Intimidation?"

"Yes."

FORTY-FOUR

THE HOTEL CONCIERGE wished Six a good evening as Six walked out into the bright streets of Harare. He had checked in using a fake name, no questions asked. He spent the rest of the afternoon going over the plans, the ones he had received from a local developer. From his calculations, he would be in and out under thirty minutes.

Six left his hotel room at 6 p.m., just before dusk. The rain had just cleared, and the sky was still overcast. He caught a taxi to Borrowdale, a rich suburb in Harare, filled with a mixture of big and small houses, both old and modern, on large pieces of land.

Twenty minutes later, Six reached the edges of the minister's mansion. The minister had seized the property from a liberation war criminal during the land reclamation program, which saw former Rhodesian settlers and their descendants give land back to the natives. The twenty-acre property was ringed with a thick hedge of cypress trees and a stone wall topped with a barbed wire coil. Six tiptoed across the road, keeping to the shadows and away from the lights and surveillance cameras. Wearing his hood and gloves, Six avoided the main entrance and instead climbed slowly over the back stone wall, as he had mapped it, and clipped the barbed wire. Two minutes later he was on the other side. Six carefully descended the wall and tiptoed into the shadows, away from the security light above the porch. He waited on the wall; his dark suit blended into the hummingbird vines that covered the wall. A guard passed by on his rounds. The guard stopped, unzipped, and took a pee. Six leaped, twisting the man in a choke hold. The guard passed out.

He dragged the guard behind trees and waited a few more seconds, making sure the coast was clear. Satisfied, he sprinted towards the baroque-style mansion with lights bright through the orchard, always keeping to the shadows. He strapped on the guard's earpiece and listened. From the voices, it seemed there were three guards remaining, two up front and one in the backyard. But he was wrong. Through the night-vision optics, he saw two guards with AK-47s station themselves at the rear door pillars. They were talking, looking in his direction. One said something into the radio, then walked the yard's perimeter.

Six stuck to his cover until the man was close, then struck him on the temple—a calculated punch that paralyzed the man. Six held the man so that he would not crumble to the ground and make noise. He dragged the unconscious man into the orchard. He waited a few more seconds. There was no movement. He proceeded.

The guard remaining was busy checking his phone when Six locked him in a stranglehold. The phone cracked on the ground as the man struggled to reach for his gun. The stranglehold immobilized the guard. Six pressed until the man was motionless and stripped him of his firearms.

Six had just finished moving that body when a fourth guard appeared, talking in his earpiece. The blow blocked any sound the man fought to emit. He lay motionless. Six pulled the unconscious body to the hedge, bound the man, and took the radio. He listened. No more voices.

The back door was unlocked. Six slowly opened it, listening for movement. He then disabled the security system. Then listened again. The only sound came from upstairs. The snoring was so loud that Six could hear it on the first floor and then on the second floor. He tiptoed up the wooden staircase, his gun outfitted with a silencer. The third floor was where all the bedrooms were located. Their doors were closed. Six sprayed concentrated chloroform under the doors.

The target's much younger wife was in the first room. His two sons were in two separate bedrooms on the east. Six felt sorry for these two boys who were to grow up without their father. The minister was sleeping in the last room on the east, the master bedroom.

The door was cracked open. Six pushed it

slowly with his foot, keeping the gun aimed and ready.

The man lay on the bed, his big belly rising and falling with the struggle of heavy breathing. Probably the reason his wife slept in another room. Maybe he'd die right then from all that fat. Six wondered what sleep was like for an evil man like the monster lying in front of him. He hoped guilt from murdering thousands of innocent people gave the man nightmares. A melatonin supplement vial sat open on the night table next to an empty glass of water. Then Six walked in, gun pointed at the man on the bed.

He looked at the minister's incapacitated body, then plunged in the needle. He felt a slight pity, then shook it off. The bastard deserved it. Those thousands of farmers—men, women, and children—deserved justice. His was the only hand to deliver that.

He waited, meanwhile observing the room. The central customized king-sized bed had golden linen that matched the golden drapes. Several eccentric pieces of artwork and carvings adorned the room, including a Zulu tribal rug hanging on the wall and a traditional ritual mask used for sacred dances. These were mixed with gilded French antiques. Six checked his fitness tracker. It was time.

Six nudged the man's face with the butt of his pistol. The minister shook. He woke up in a sweat, in a nightmare. He wiped his eyes. The nightmare was scary. He couldn't run. He remembered a creepy story his grandmother told him. Satisfied it was only a dream, he reached over to turn on the light. His arm wouldn't move. He struggled, groaning. *Heart attack again?* He looked at the golden cross placed opposite his bed, offering a silent prayer.

"Hello, Mr. Matsanga."

Matsanga paused, making sure he heard well. His head always played tricks on him. He mapped, gazed around the room, adjusting to the darkness, finally seeing a silhouette figure of a man, all in black, and masked. He scrambled for the security caller. But his hands remained stiff, like stumps. His mind willed his arm to move, but his muscles had other ideas. He was awake and it was horror.

"Having a nice dream?"

Matsanga's eyes opened wider. Sleep gone.

"Don't bother. It doesn't work."

"What have you done to me?"

"Painful, isn't it? Being powerless. I'm doing what you've done to thousands of innocent people. Farmers, women, children. How it felt when you brutally murdered them, harvested their organs, raped them. How does it feel to know that your life is in someone else's hands?"

"You'll pay!"

"Save your breath. You have about fifteen minutes to live. The injection will make sure that happens. You'll see your life escaping from your body slowly and painfully, and you cannot do anything about it. I want you to think about all those girls and boys your men took. All those kids you forced into child soldiers, stripping away their future. All those villages you burned, women, children, young, old."

"You have the wrong man."

"Right now, your body has lost all function in your extremities. One by one your limbs are becoming useless, and eventually your brain will lose oxygen and you will hallucinate, then as an extra measure you will have cardiac arrest."

"I'm the minister of—"

"Yes, you are. But let me finish first. You feel the pain, don't you? Don't worry, your brain and nervous system are perfectly functional, and you will feel every ounce of pain and emotion from our little session."

Wide, terrified eyes stared back at Six.

"Just imagine the headline: Fat minister dies of a heart attack." He paused. "No one will question that. Just like that, you will be forgotten. The empire you have been building for yourself will be gone."

The man stared at the ceiling with bloodshot eyes.

"Tell me one thing, why did you do it? All those people?"

"I am not telling you anything."

"Twelve minutes now." Six rose, unlocked his phone, and showed the man a video of his wife and children in bed.

The man's head bobbed up and down.

"You will die for your sins. The only way you will save them is to tell me the truth. And only the truth shall save them."

The man's mouth opened to protest.

"And that depends on how convincing your story is. If I don't believe it, each one of them will get a bullet." Six retrieved his pistol and smelled it.

The man shook.

"Let me tell you how this is going to work," Six said, squeezing a little more of the syringe into Matsanga's immobilized arm.

"This soluble isotope, half-life six hours. By the time your boys and wife wake up, you won't be here, and the drug will be cleared from your system, and you know what everyone will say. You should have had that heart of yours checked."

Six pointed to the French gilded bronze pedestal clock opposite the bed. The old man's terrified gaze ran to the clock.

"Heart failure, excruciating cramps. You can feel the pain and can still talk. I want you to feel the pain of all those men, those women, those children that you and your men murdered."

The man was sweating profusely as he struggled to scream.

"No one will hear you. Your family is asleep. Who knows, I might have some fun with them after."

"Will you let my family live if I give you what you want?"

"Yes."

"How can I trust you?"

"You've my word. I'm sure they are as innocent as everyone else. You are my primary target. From the way things are now, your life hangs on a balance, and you can save them." The minister named names. He told Six about his safe at National Bank. "All evidence is there," he croaked, struggling to breathe.

Six unlocked the man's phone and transferred its files to the cloud. He said, "I hope you rot in hell."

Six walked to the massive mahogany door. He watched as the old man struggled as the toxin stiffened his limbs and his heart stopped.

Five hours later, Six was in bed back in Vic Falls. He slept for two hours, got up, and headed down to the cafeteria to grab some coffee. The phone showed three missed calls from Reggie. He called back.

"Thank God you are okay," he said.

"Do you see the news? The minister is dead. Reports say he died of a heart attack."

"One less evil man in the world."

"Anything you want to tell me?"

"No."

"Meet here at the office at eleven."

"I'll see you there."

CHAPTER
FORTY-FIVE

WHILE THEY WERE CONFERRING at the station, Six's phone beeped. Reggie asked what it was. Then Six told her what he had been doing.

"I copied everything from Liu's computer, and my guy at NEPHRON sorted it out. Guess Liu delegated the auctioning role to his sidekick."

"What did you find?" Reggie said.

"We intercepted the form of communication between the minister and his band of clients for the upcoming auction. Using files I collected from Liu's desk, I was able to gain access to the secure channel. I paid a $200,000 deposit to start bidding for two females and four males. They are the cover for what the participants are calling 'the prize.' All their communication is done on the dark web, a trashy site, easier to overlook if you don't know what you are looking for."

"And you were able to do this?"

"Not me, but there are people in my organization who do this kind of stuff 24/7. Turns out all participants have anime characters as avatars. We were able to partly decode from the character's character, which reflects the person on the other side. Except for the Lion King. He is undoubtedly the ringleader."

"So have you identified them?"

"No, but we are hoping the trail of messages will allow us to decode where the meeting will be, hopefully. Most of the messages are metaphors. We need to find who the Lion King is. I know the minister was in on it. His was the mongoose character. His avatar had stopped sending messages, and that was bad, because he was the one driving the bidding. We hacked into his phone and we are now sending messages on his behalf, as the mongoose."

"So what's the game plan?"

"To get them to commit more and more money, then freeze the funds," Six said.

"How much has been bid so far?"

"Two billion dollars."

"You're kidding."

"No." He showed the screen to Reggie.

"There are people with that kind of money to throw around on the dark web?"

"You bet. For immortality! That's the prize."

"And people believe that bullshit?" Reggie said.

"The fun. The risk. The leap of faith," Six said.

"I guess when you have all that cash, you can have any experience you desire."

"Including bidding for the elixir of life."

They laughed.

FORTY-SIX

SIX GOT breakfast and scrolled through his phone, and again met with Reggie at the station, in a room now converted into an investigation zone.

"I think we found the head of the snake," Six said.

"Who?"

"This guy!"

Six showed Reggie the picture. "My intel tells me this guy is at the helm," Six said.

"That's Hellstrom, the philanthropist," Reggie said.

"That may explain why he was interested in Professor de Klerk's research. I convinced one of my guys at the agency to look more into it. My agency hacked into some of his accounts. Turns out some of them have been linked to organized crime and trafficking rampant in East and Central Africa, often funding several warlords like Kony and the D.R.C."

Lin walked in. Reggie and Six brought her up to date.

"Hellstrom. The Dutch billionaire."

"You know him?"

"Not personally," said Lin, "but the MI6 has been after him for a while. He is a slippery snake. We have been monitoring his companies for a while. Mr. Hellstrom is involved in illegal trading and sponsoring guns for civil wars. Recent intel points to him being a leader of a crime ring, bigger than we anticipated. Kickbacks, shady doings, poaching for ivory, ammunition, anything to destabilize the economies in African countries he does business."

"I was just explaining to Reggie that we were able to hack into Liu's phone, which allowed me access to the dark club, the immortality club."

"What is that?"

"An illegal website actioning rare African artifacts. And young kids. The users use aliases, of course, but I was able to trace it to the minister. Even the most meticulous criminals make a mistake at some point."

"I think we found the Lion King." Reggie said. When Lin looked confused, she said, "That's the name of the character who we thought was the leader."

"How were you able to get in?"

"I'm one of the bidders," said Six.

"Aren't there restrictions?"

"No, you just need $200,000 to register for a chance to bid."

"They could still trace your identity," Lin said.

"This is the dark web we are talking about. None of the bidders know who the others are."

"Lin, anything else from your side that might be helpful?"

"Our assets on the ground say he will be at his mountain villa in Switzerland this weekend."

"Positive?"

"He goes there every summer."

"Why Switzerland?"

"Favorable taxes. He's rich. Plus he is a philanthropist."

"Bullshit. Most of these givers usually use that as a cover for unscrupulous activities."

"As a penance for their evil, I guess," Reggie said.

"Our people could try to get him," said Lin. "But it will take years. Too much bureaucracy. The paperwork itself will require harvesting all trees in the Amazon forest."

"Try other, not in line, methods," Six said. "Like going to Switzerland."

"I won't let you do that," Lin said.

"Try me. I don't work for MI6. I'm a ghost."

"Then I'm coming with you."

"No, it's too dangerous."

"If I feared danger, I'd not be in this job."

"Okay. I guess I will need someone to cover my back," Six said.

"I got you. Look, we've been after this guy for years."

"Where do we start?"

"We leave tomorrow morning."

"Our intel says he is already in Europe, so that will work," Lin said. "Zurich."

"I should've known. Where else would an unscrupulous businessman hide in the world?" Reggie said.

"Where did you get your intel?" asked Six.

"Okay, since we don't have time to waste, the minister told me."

"The dead minister?" Reggie said.

Lin said, "Don't tell me you—"

"I did," Six said. "I paid your boyfriend a visit last night to have a chat."

Lin glared at Six from across the table. "Do you see what you did? You jeopardized our whole mission. Years of work gone to waste."

"Well, sorry. The International Criminal Court is not my M.O. We could wait while you two drank pina coladas and fine-dined. But I've a local family waiting to hear answers to why and who killed their father and husband. I had to get answers now."

"Oh, God!"

"I like to get things done," Six said. "What did you want? Send the guy to prison? He sits like a king for a few weeks, then walks free on a million-dollar bail, and then it's business as usual. None of the victims ever get restitution."

"So you're the judge now?"

"I just eliminate bad guys. No more, no less."

"What happens if they find out it was murder?" Reggie said.

"They won't."

"How're you so sure?"

"That's why I did not want to kill the guards. I also wanted to make sure the minister's death would look like an accident. Neither the guards nor the family will remember what happened. The guy already had heart problems."

"We are all after the same thing," Reggie said. "Obviously, this is bigger than any of us thought. We have to work together," she said.

"I had him where I wanted him," Lin said. "Now all my work is ruined."

"Not really," Six said. "You have what was on his phone. That will keep The Hague busy for a while."

"So. What else did you find?"

"The guy called Lion King has properties in Dallas and Miami."

"Houses?"

"Yeah. Average ten million dollars. It's a common tax strategy used by the wealthy to write-off mortgage interest on their income taxes. Plus, states like Texas do not have state property taxes. None of them were under his name, but under a shell company that our guys have been trying to untangle."

"An easy multimillion-dollar investment with a massive tax write-off," Lin said.

"Exactly."

Lin took out a thumb drive and inserted it into Reggie's computer, and opened a series of files, showing the minister's phone records, recordings, contracts, payments in the billions. The file also listed several offshore shell accounts and properties in Switzerland and Malta.

"What's the legal way to get to the Lion King?" asked Reggie.

"See if we can follow the money trail to

more fish," said Lin. "At least one of them will want to see Hellstrom in jail."

Six's phone buzzed.

"Our intelligence confirms he will be in Zurich tomorrow."

"We go to Zurich, then."

"I can't," Reggie said. "My work is to find the missing kids."

"Lin and I can go. We can use you here on the ground," Six said. His phone buzzed again, and Six looked at it. "My contact will meet me in Porto, this afternoon, with everything we need," Six said.

CHAPTER
FORTY-SEVEN

THE UBER PICKED up Six and Lin at the Porto train station. The hotel was fifteen minutes away. They had plenty of time to kill. After changing into fresh clothes and checking the room, Six made sure to leave items aligned, in case someone invaded the room. He marveled at the ornamented ceiling, painted in the 1900s. The cozy, Victorian old-school furnishings, mirrors, desk, tiled sink, and bathtub. Victorian charm. Everything purple and velvety. The room oozed purple and royalty.

The hotel overlooked the shoreline, opposite Vila Nova de Gaia, a hub for oligarchs dodging taxes in their home countries. Portugal was known for its affordable living.

They drank coffee and walked to the park, lush and colorful, with multitudes picnicking and others people-watching. They sat down next to the fountain. Lin looked svelte in the flowered dress she chose and the white laced sandals. She wore a verandah straw hat, purchased at the airport. Six chose khaki cargo shorts, an Oxford long-sleeved shirt rolled up to the elbows, moccasins, and cheap sunglasses he had bought at a flea market. They also bought dried fruits and pastries.

"So what's up with you and Reggie?" asked Lin. "Are you guys an item?"

"We're just working together."

Lin smiled. "Really?"

Six looked at her inquisitively.

"I have spent my entire career studying people. And I can see there is more. The chemistry between you two is obvious."

"Isn't that what work partners should be?"

"Yes and no. Yours is on a different level."

"I think you are mistaken. We are just doing a job."

"Just doing a job?"

"Yes, just a job. Our ride is here. I'd much rather prefer it to the fun that's waiting for us on the other side."

He pointed to the bright Vila Nova de Gaia shoreline, lined with massive yachts.

Lin hooked her arm across his. "I'm just passing on my naïve observations."

Six helped her into the river taxi. On the river's other side, hand in hand, they wove through bistro tables packed with diners, all along the shoreline. They joined a woman sitting at a table alone sipping on a pina colada, wearing all-black attire, with a white blouse and thick red lipstick. She smiled as they sat down. Six drew a chair for Lin.

The woman eyed Lin.

"Can we trust her?" the woman finally said.

"Yes. This is agent Lin I told you about. MI6."

"If you trust her, I trust her too."

The server arrived. Both Lin and Six ordered pina coladas.

"This is my favorite," the woman said.

"Mine as well," Lin said.

They waited for the waiter to leave.

"So what do we have?" Six said.

"Our sources report that Hellstrom will be staying at the Bau au Lac."

"Are you positive?" Six said.

"Yes," the woman said. "The hotel is very discreet about their high-profile clients, but we have other ways of getting information."

"How many days?"

"We don't know, except that tomorrow evening is a positive."

"So we have to take care of business tomorrow?"

"Yes. You have one night to get everything taken care of."

Six nodded.

The woman reached into her leather purse, retrieved two folders, and handed each one to Six and Lin.

"There is all the information you will need. Your itinerary, details, train tickets, passports, and flight out of Zurich."

Lin and Six opened the folders.

"You will go there as newlyweds. Mr. and Mrs. Draye and Kai George. A well-off couple."

"Everything is set. You will stay at the suite

adjacent to the presidential suite where we know Hellstrom will be staying. Memorize everything in that packet that pertains to your identity on this trip."

"Thanks," Six and Lin replied in unison.

The woman rose and left. The waiter brought the drinks.

"You're a tech startup founder, huh?" Lin said, sipping on the drink.

"Gotta start acting like one. I don't even use social media."

"I can teach you."

"Merci beaucoup! And you're a socialite."

"I can be one," Lin said, pausing and making faces. "I just need the cameras and the paparazzi."

"Of course."

"Look at this ring!" Lin said, sliding a large diamond ring onto her wedding finger.

"Definitely shouts 'filthy rich.'"

"Why the train? I hate overnight train rides."

"Less scrutiny. We are carrying some dangerous stuff. And this is Switzerland. Who wouldn't want to sail through the Alps in the train at this time of the year? I think it's going to be awesome."

"I know it will be."

CHAPTER
FORTY-EIGHT

THE TRAIN REACHED Zurich early in the morning. Lin and Six spent a major portion of the trip not sightseeing but sleeping. The room had been comfortable, with bunk beds.

The hotel was beautiful, having been built in the early nineteenth century. The Swiss government had named it a historic site. A sign was prominently displayed near the front entrance, listing all the facts about the place. They entered the building hand in hand. The lobby ceiling was covered with a seventeenth-century-style mural commissioned by the founder of the hotel. Several sculptures including a fifteenth-century full steel plate armor and long swords in scabbards neatly lined the lounge. There were portraits of notable celebrities, national leaders, including a former U.S. president who had stayed there, and some British royalty.

The keys to the third-floor suite were old-school, bronze, from back when the hotel was built. The doors were heavy pine. The room was warm, with a French royalty feel to everything, purple and gold colors in one form or another. The carpet, bed, linen, curtains, chairs, faucets, everything. The room offered stunning 180-degree views of the Zurich Lake and the Alps. Six thought it must cost a fortune to stay here. Several paintings adorned the walls. A customized card welcomed Mr. and Mrs. George to the hotel. Rose petals sprinkled into a heart shape lay on the bed. A wine bottle was on the desk in the ice bucket.

Lin looked at its label. "Nineteen thirty-eight Chateau Latour!" Lin said. "Do you know how much this cost?"

"Fifty dollars," Six said.

"Three thousand!"

"Damn!" Six said. "Now we definitely need to drink it."

Lin laughed, removed the cork with a corkscrew, then filled two flutes. They clinked the glasses.

"To drinking the most expensive wine."

They laughed.

They spent the rest of the day planning, going over plans, and setting up their equipment and listening devices. Six's contact had supplied the layout of the hotel in case of an emergency, if they had to run for it. Both Six and Lin hoped they would not have to.

Six killed time flipping through TV channels, occasionally settling on a soccer game.

Hellstrom's motorcade arrived at 4 p.m.

"They are here," Lin said, peeping through the window.

The pair watched Hellstrom and the rest of the entourage roll into the drop-off arc and disappear into the lobby. They both checked everything again. All devices were working. Time to get to work. The first order of business was for Lin to meet them in the elevator. Lin, dressed in a glossy rose dress and sporting her large diamond ring, waited in the elevator, and exited while Hellstrom got out, surrounded by four well-dressed men. He smiled at Lin, who smiled back.

"Positive. Target positive," Lin said, when the elevator door closed behind her.

"Copy that," Six said.

Now that they knew Hellstrom was there, the waiting game resumed. They listened. Hellstrom, a busy man, had a strictly structured schedule. Six's contact had provided them with a tentative schedule for Hellstrom's day. They hoped it had not changed. He was scheduled to go to dinner at 8 p.m., then an opera at the Zurich Opera House.

At eight, the doors from the other room opened, and Hellstrom left.

"Target on the move," Six said.

"Copy that," Lin said. She was sitting at the bar by the lobby, drinking hot chocolate while pretending to read a magazine. She watched the same group of four men, then Hellstrom, descend the stairs, wave to the concierge, and board two SUVs waiting outside.

"Target is off."

"Copy that. Hurry."

"I'm on it."

Lin waited for several minutes, chatted with the bartender, then went back to the suite.

Six was already waiting. They strode along the hallway hand in hand, making sure none of the other guests saw them, then turned right directly to the presidential suite. Because of the hotel's exclusivity and for the secrecy of their high-profile clients, one policy of the hotel was to not include cameras inside or outside of rooms. One selling point was that within these hotel walls anyone could do what they wanted, and they never left a trace.

They put on masks and gloves. Six took a key in his pocket and slid it into the heavy wooden door. It clicked, and he pushed the door open.

They checked several spots for cameras. The window, the faucets, wall clock, wall paintings. They found nothing.

"Great," Six said.

"Try the safe, while I check the bags and drawers," Lin said.

"Copy that."

They went to work.

Six was glad to find a modern safe. He used his decoding device to trace the keys on the safe, which would take approximately five minutes. He then joined Lin in the bedroom, going through the shelves and carefully putting things back as they had found them. They found an appointment book. Lin snapped photos of all the pages.

They moved on to the closet. Nothing. Then next, the living room. While they were in the kitchen, they heard the elevator chime. Lin tiptoed to and looked through the peephole.

"He is back!" she said, while tiptoeing, and hid behind the sofa.

Six hid in the closet. The door swung open, and Hellstrom, with two of his men, walked in. He took off his jacket and waistcoat, slumped onto the sofa, and turned on the TV. After a few minutes he went to the bathroom, newspaper in hand.

Six checked the time. Thirty seconds till the safe unlocked. He was unsure whether the device would make a noise when it matched the code. But he didn't want to take any chances. The two men in the room stood waiting, looking around for a while, then one then sat on the couch while the other remained standing.

With fifteen seconds to go, Six leaped, catching the standing man on the jaw, crashing into his earpiece. On cue, Lin managed to chokehold the man on the couch. The couch tumbled backward, but she did not let go as the man elbowed her and kicked until froth came out of his mouth and nose.

Six's man tried reaching for his gun, which Six kicked out of his hand. He caught Six with a side hook which sent Six tumbling onto the table. The man leaped towards Six. Six rolled to the side just in time and cut the man's legs from under him, and the man banged on the hardwood. Six jumped and planted the blade, severing the man's trachea as he tried to talk.

Six checked the watch. Ten seconds.

"Two more outside," Lin said.

They heard footsteps. The men called several times before unlocking the door, guns drawn.

The safe beeped and clicked loudly.

Six and Lin had been ready, standing behind the door. Moving as one, they dislodged the men's guns and sent them tumbling to the floor. Lin followed with a flying kick that crashed into one man's skull. The other man flung a knife. Noticing his dead comrades and realizing he was outmatched, he threw another blade at Six. The knife whizzed past as Hellstrom was coming out of the bathroom. Hellstrom did not see what was coming and had zero chance to react.

"What was—?" The knife sank into his collarbone before he finished the question. He stood there momentarily shocked, mouth and eyes wide open in horror, then grabbed at the knife as he stumbled to the sofa. Blood clogged his mouth and windpipe. He coughed blood, struggling for words. The serrated blade pulled with it flesh and bone fragments as he struggled to extract it.

At the same time, Lin pinned the remaining bodyguard to the wall, using one of the other guard's knives.

Lin and Six rushed to Hellstrom, who was now gasping for his last breath, struggling to call for help. Lin placed a few rugs on his chest and tried to revive him, to no avail.

"He's done!" Six grabbed a bag from the opened safe. "We have everything that we need. Let's go."

"Shit! What are we going to do about him?"

•   •   •

SIX AND LIN had breakfast at the hotel café. They watched as everything resumed normally. About 9:30 a.m., they noticed a few policemen make their way into the hotel quietly. Six and Lin exchanged glances.

"They are discreet. They don't want to freak out the rest of their clients."

"How do you think it will go?"

"They will probably say he died of a heart attack."

"No one who saw him would believe that."

"Old money likes to keep things private. His family would probably want to keep this to themselves, rather than to let the paparazzi have a feast."

They stood. Six kissed Lin's hand. They walked out of the lobby hand in hand. They waved at the concierge, who had a bellhop wheel over and load their suitcases.

"Bon voyage!" the concierge said.

FORTY-NINE

HELLSTROM'S DEATH was highly publicized, leaving the Swiss government searching for answers. The official cause was a stroke. The press was feasting on speculations. Pundits weighed in on the mysterious death of the renowned philanthropist. The world was shocked as more and more facts about the beloved deceased billionaire came to light. Many felt his good deeds atoned for his sins, yet many more believed he deserved his death. All wondered who had killed him. Was it the CIA, MI6? Was this a warning sign to other corrupt business leaders who thought they were invincible?

Some of the evidence Six and Lin had recovered from the safe went to HQ, and the rest to MI6, which froze all of Hellstrom's accounts. Lin's agency had implicated several Anglo-American steel and mining corporations on charges ranging from illegal weapons, kickbacks, and tax evasion, all webbed in offshore shell accounts. A military-industrial complex. Several

German companies would be charged for illegal arms delivered to Mozambique. Several companies would be taken to the international court. Most of the credit went to the MI6. Instead of returning to London, Lin insisted on going back to Victoria Falls with Six. "My job there is not done," she told Six.

"That's another ten years of trial by the international court. The victims would be lucky to get a cent of the resources that's been looted from them," Six said to Lin.

"Nothing here has changed," Lin said. "The mayor has taken the minister's place as well as Liu's. He's enjoying it. Wish I could choke the life out of that schmuck!"

REGGIE HAD JUST FINISHED MEDITATING and was ready to go to bed when her phone rang. She checked the caller I.D. Unknown.

"Hello?"

"May I speak to Reggie?"

"Who's this?"

"Celia. I'm a nurse at the regional hospital."

Reggie's heart raced. "This is Reggie."

"I've a patient here who wants to talk to you."

"Reggie," said a familiar voice.

"Clive! What's going on? Are you okay?"

"Can you come to the hospital?"

"Sure, I'm on my way now."

Five minutes later, Reggie pulled into the parking lot at the regional hospital. The receptionist directed her to Room 25 after she flashed her badge. The elevator was taking forever. She sprinted up the stairs. Clive, heavily bandaged, was hooked to intravenous lines, both of blood and saline. He forced a smile, then winced because of his cracked lips.

"What happened?"

"Drank a little too much, and the only thing I remember is being in this hospital."

"Don't talk too much," the nurse said. She looked at Reggie. "He lost a lot of blood. Lots of water in his lungs. Two broken ribs."

"Almost drowned?"

"Water interrogation possibility. Airway tissue lining damage from forced breathing."

Reggie said, "Do you remember what happened?"

"Fragments. Drinking, losing consciousness, being dipped in water head down, and being punched."

Reggie stared at him.

"Last thing I remember were the guards receiving a phone call, the room filling with hysteria, and everyone deserted, leaving only the junior guard. I was so out of it. Next thing I know, I was here."

The nurse said, "The guard said someone in a truck dropped him at the main entrance and left."

"Did he identify the person?"

"A female all in black. About five foot six."

The drugs the nurse injected kicked in, and Clive was again sedated.

Reggie called Six. "I'm at the hospital with Clive. He is in serious condition. I'll explain it to you in person." After hanging up, Reggie phoned the station and requested an officer to guard Clive's hospital room.

REGGIE AND SIX stood watching Clive, his chest rising and falling slowly, and the beeping of the EKG and several screens around the bed. Lin joined them at the hospital.

Reggie felt Clive's forehead.

"The nurse says he will be okay," she said.

"I'm sure he will get through it."

"What was he doing?"

"Alcohol. He probably pissed off the wrong people."

Lin had agreed to meet them at the hospital to share recent developments.

"How's your other partner, by the way?" Lin said to Six, looking at Reggie.

"It was you, wasn't it? You dropped Clive at the hospital."

"He should thank me for being there in time before the guy put a bullet through his head."

"How did you find him?"

"I saw him by chance being dragged into a van from the pub. And followed them. I have been on these guys for a while. Found him in that abandoned tobacco shed just outside the city."

"He was talking to Liu's crew?"

"Yes. Things didn't go so well. The other guys were mad. And they dragged him out."

"I'm surprised they didn't kill him."

"Maybe they didn't want to. They just wanted to teach him a lesson. I think they were interrupted. I was late to get to them, but they left in a rush. One guy got a call, and they all rushed back into SUVs and left."

"Did you see what the vehicles looked like?"

"Cadillac Escalades. The ones the mayor uses."

"Maybe he owed the mayor's guys a debt or something," Reggie said.

"I think Clive was supplying info to Liu, and then to his crew," Six said.

Reggie seemed shocked. Then she said, "I feel like a fool. You told me before that Clive might be the one selling us out. And I didn't believe you," Reggie said.

"It just means you're a good person," Six said, placing his hand on hers. "You believe in the good in people. And that's a good thing."

"But people take advantage of that."

"Some people will."

"I can't believe this."

"Just take it easy," Six said. "Clive will tell us more when he wakes up."

"How did you know he was the mole?" Reggie said.

"My gut told me, the first time I saw him.

But after I talked to you, I set up Clive with false information. I also deliberately kept false evidence at the station of our findings. Evidence at the station was tampered with. My intuition told me Clive couldn't be trusted. The only reason there were fewer guards at Liu's is because I had let some false plans slip. Clive heard that and alerted Liu. Worked out to our advantage."

"Always wondered why these guys were a step ahead of us," Reggie said.

"I gave Clive false information the night we rescued the girls at the warehouse, which had made Liu divert most of his guards."

"They probably beat him for supplying false information."

"Clive was the only other person who knew that you had talked to Louis. They beat him up before we could question him."

Reggie raged. "So they were always ahead of us."

"Clive was giving them updates on our plans. That's also why I did some things on my own. I understood you couldn't keep some things from your partner.

"You remember when Clive arrived at the office before his shift started? That sudden change in patterns just doesn't happen. He was curious to see what you would do after you got the note."

"Do you think he did something to the safari guide?"

"I don't know," Six said. "But they killed Louis after he talked to us. I can presume Clive told them that as well."

"That's why he was discouraging us from pursuing the mayor, and to focus on the kids."

"Yes. He was adamant about not going to the minister's house as well."

"I'll be damned!"

"Clive has always been dragging the whole thing from the start."

Reggie said, "We will let the man himself tell us why."

FIFTY-TWO

CLIVE HAD JUST WOKEN up and saw Six and Lin as well as a furious Reggie in his room.

"You want to explain what happened?"

Clive's eyes tracked across the room from Six, to Lin, then fixed on Reggie. Six and Lin got the message and left the room.

"I'm sorry, I screwed up."

"Screwed up? You have a funny way of looking at things."

"I know alright. I messed everything up."

"You almost had me killed!"

"Reggie, I'm sorry."

"What happened to partnership? Having each other's back? The badge to fight corruption."

A tear cascaded down Clive's cheekbone. "I didn't have a choice."

"You always have a choice."

"I don't know what I was thinking. By the time I wanted out, I was in too deep."

"How did you get tangled up with these guys?"

"Started one night with a couple of drinks and extra favors."

"You have a family, man. You gotta man up."

Clive looked at the ceiling, tears still falling. "I know. My wife and kids would be ashamed of me. I don't know why I did this. They were going to kill me, but a phone call came that save my life. I only remember sounds, glares, shadows of cars leaving, then I must have passed out after that."

"Did you have anything to do with Louis or the safari guide's death?"

Clive remained quiet, tears still cascading.

"The guide had a family too! Did that ever cross your mind, or your selfishness didn't even think of that?"

"What did you want me to do?"

"What do they have on you?"

"My family."

"Why didn't you tell me?"

"I couldn't. I'm already a dead man for saying this."

"Blue blood, remember? We stay together."

"This country has corrupted many minds. I wanted to be a good cop, you know. But we get paid peanuts. And I've seven children. School is not free. These are confusing times. Don't know what's right or wrong. So I drink."

"But your children need you. Your wife needs you."

"What should I do?"

"You can still do the right thing. It's never too late," she said. "I know you have a way out. You didn't just blindly do this with no way out."

"Man, I'm dead!"

"No," Reggie said. "Not if you do exactly as I say. Hold back nothing."

"Okay," he said. "Are my kids going to be safe?"

"I'm sending guards there now," Reggie said.

"I've all the evidence you need at the bank, secured. There is everything these guys have ever done; names, aliases," said Clive.

"That should work."

"Can you give me and Six a min?" Clive said.

Reggie stepped out of the room and told Six to go in

"Look, man," Clive said. "I know I've been a dick to you. I'm sorry."

"It's alright, man. Just focus on getting better."

"I didn't mean for you or anyone to get hurt."

"We all make mistakes."

"So you're not mad?"

"No. I know how it feels. You and Reggie have been partners for years, and I stepped into your shoes."

"Yeah. I was once a good cop. I screwed up badly."

"I know you're not as naïve as you pretend to be. You must have an alibi, or hid something in case things went south."

Clive stared at Six.

"You have nothing to lose by telling all," Six said. "Your family is safe. The only thing you can do right now is to do the right thing. For your family, and that badge. For Reggie, who almost got killed."

"But my family?"

"The sooner we get these guys, the safer you and your family will be. You know they will not stop coming after you. You don't really have much of a choice. Are you going to let a lot of innocent people die for nothing?"

Clive closed his eyes for a moment.

"Can you get Reggie in?"

Six opened the door and called Reggie.

Clive gave them the actual coordinates Liu had the mayor focused on. He didn't know exactly what was there, but one day Liu forgot to secure his phone and Clive took a photo.

"Are you sure that's the main thing?"

"I know it is. Liu said it was important. I think it is what you're looking for. The coordinates must mean something."

"And where is this map?"

"In a folder on a secure server at the station."

"Smart."

"I didn't want to keep it in my phone because I had a feeling all our phones were bugged. They could search my phone anytime."

"Okay," Six said. "Let's see how honest you are. Give me the password."

Six thanked Clive and filed out. The officer at the door acknowledged him. He had a reputation now in town.

CHAPTER
FIFTY-THREE

THE COORDINATES LED them to the center of the jungle, not far from the Khoisan cave. Six, Reggie, Lin, and six officers Reggie had recruited from the station, keeping the mission under the radar, had loaded their firearms. They parked the safari cruisers. They had brought more than enough firepower, just in case. There were wild animals as well as other things to worry about.

Six surveyed the area. He chose the sniper rifle, and strapped on two SIG pistols, one on the chest pouch, over the bulletproof vest, and another on the pouch strapped around his thigh. The rest of the crew strapped their own ammunition.

"This is the place," Six said. "That's what the coordinates say."

"Let's just hope the messages you got from your dark web chat were accurate," said Reggie. "Otherwise, the chief will roast me when he finds I recruited officers behind his back."

"All the stakeholders should be meeting here. The stakeholders who are not dead yet."

"Someone has been here recently," said Lin. "There is a tire trail."

"Let's split up."

"I don't think we can trust Clive's information," Lin said.

Six said, "The man has gone through hell. Almost died. I don't see why he would give us false info given the situation."

"Whatever loyalty he thought he had before is gone now."

"Loyalty in the Mafia. They are power games. You just hope today is not your day," Reggie said, and as soon as she finished speaking, a bullet rang out and hit the officer next to her. The man's head exploded.

"Shit! We got company!" she yelled, returning fire. Then everyone dove for cover and lay flat behind the trucks in the grass.

"How's the officer?"

"He's dead."

"Where did that come from?"

"West," one of the officers said, pointing to the woods.

"Great. How are we going to see someone there?"

"The sniper is camouflaged."

"They were ready."

Several more rounds fired, smashing and shattering the windscreens for two of the vehicles, popping one tire. Six lay flat with his sniper rifle, mapping the woods. He cracked one shot. A man fell from the trees. Several more bullets whizzed from multiple directions. Six fired several shots, plucking the souls of his targets one by one. Yells ricocheted in the forest.

"We don't know how many are in there! We have to move!" Six shouted.

"We can't drive out of here. Whoever is shooting has higher ground and can pick us off, one by one, like chickens."

"Let's split up. Reggie, you and your guard go that way. Lin and your guys that way. You two guys are coming with me. Cover me, then we will cover you once we reach the woods."

Reggie and Lin opened fire with their assault rifles as Six and two officers sprinted forward. In a few seconds the trio had reached the woods and positioned themselves against the trees.

"In position now," Six said into his headset.

"Copy that." Reggie responded.

Six sprayed the undergrowth with a rifle. He hit a man covered in leaves. The man screamed.

"One down."

Six's team opened fire while Lin and Reggie and their officers scrambled towards the woods. Several bullets ricocheted in the trees. The team fired back. An officer on Lin's team yelped.

"Man down," Lin said.

"Keep moving. Fan out."

Gunfire continued for several minutes, then ceased. Reggie tore the sleeve off her shirt and bandaged Lin's shoulder; she had been hit in the triceps.

"We got them all. Let's move in!" As Six spoke, another bullet whizzed by.

Six emptied his magazine in the bullet's direction, flipped, and reloaded. The man yelped and fell.

"Never say 'we got them all'," an officer cautioned Six. "Whatever it is, they are defending it to the death."

They moved forward, sweeping the area clean with rifle fire.

This far into the jungle, network communications were intermittent. Six radioed, "We've found a structure," and Lin and Reggie and their teams, while staying hidden, moved closer.

"It's concrete and gated. We have to go in."

"Copy that," Lin and Reggie said.

They heard no more from Six except gunfire.

Six swept his gun from side to side, catching a man hiding behind the structure's wall. A bullet ricocheted off the concrete wall, hitting one of Six's officers in the neck. Six and the other officer returned fire. Six, now very angry, switched to the SIG pistol and moved forward. At the bolted metal barricade Six opened the lock by shooting it.

The structure concealed the entrance to a tunnel. The area inside it was well lit.

Six keyed the radio.

"We are in! Reggie, do you copy?"

There was no response. He checked the bars on his phone. There were none.

"I guess it's just us!"

Six and the officer stayed glued to the wall for cover.

"Don't kill us!" faint voices echoed.

Six and his officer paused.

"Did you hear that?"

The officer nodded, and called out "Police!"

"Help us! Please!"

Six hurried forward over the rocky earth, his rifle on the ready. The tunnel opened out, and at the center was a cage holding the six missing kids.

"Cover me," Six said to the officer.

Quickly, he shot the bolts of the locks, releasing the kids. Some cried with relief. There were two girls and four boys. Six recognized one of the boys.

"Anyone else here?" Six did not wait for an answer. "Jadin, I remember you from the cafeteria. We need to get you out of here."

A shot rang out. A man fell from the roof of the tunnel. Six looked back at the officer, whose gun was still smoking.

"Thank you!" Six said. He turned. "Listen! Jadin, you're the quarterback. You gotta lead your team out."

"What about him?" the girl said, pointing to the farther end of the tunnel, where a path led to another open chamber.

"Who is there?"

"The thing. It's chained up."

"Get the kids out of here and away," Six told his officers.

Six, on high alert, walked forward into the chamber where *Nyaminyami* was strapped. He had never seen anything like it before. The creature resembled an eel, with tentacles that resembled a slug, with a metal muzzle strapped to its mouth.

The slug-eel creature was suspended a few meters off the ground with chains.

"I got you," Six said. Immediately the creature bellowed and heaved, causing the cage and straps to vibrate. The whole tunnel shook.

Six looked the creature in the eyes. "Come on, I'm just here to help."

He aimed his pistol at the bindings, breaking one at a time. Six shots later, the creature tumbled to the ground. The muzzle fell to the side. After several moments, the creature blinked, finding it was free. Then it rose, thudding, roaring, sending shards of rock and shrapnel everywhere. It shot an electric current bolt towards Six. Six dove to the side just in time. The wall tumbled.

It heaved forward and glided past him, trailing water, toward the exit. Without hesitation, Six rose and followed it. The creature bounced into a wall. Immediately fog and water filled the area. The water level was rising fast. There was no way out except through the metal barricade. The creature lurched forward on a wave of water and pounced on the broken barricade. Immediately water stopped gushing, and the earth absorbed what water there was. Then it slithered on its belly into the jungle and did not look back, and now it was quiet.

"You're welcome," Six said. Then he remembered.

"Hey, kids," he shouted. "Reggie! Everybody! It's over!"

Then the rocks behind him gave way. An avalanche of mud and rocks poured in, slamming Six flat. His life flashed before his eyes.

It was over.

FIFTY-FOUR

SIX WOKE UP. Reggie was kneeling beside him.

"What happened?"

"Lie down," she said, placing a hand on his stomach.

Six groaned. "Lin?"

"She's fine." Reggie pointed to the other ambulance.

Reggie summoned the medic who had just arrived.

"I think I broke a rib or something."

The medic strapped the gas on him, and he drifted to sleep.

FIFTY-FIVE

CLIVE WAS FOUND DEAD, and one of the officers who guarded his hospital room was shot dead.

Reggie punched the brick wall after hearing the news. She phoned the medical examiner.

"Same drug overdose found in the last victim. Triple Z," Joyce told Reggie. "My best guess would be through the drips. But none of the drips or tubing had been punctured."

"So how?"

"That's the million-dollar question. We use disposable drips. Each device used is unpacked from a sterile package for use. Just once for each patient. We no longer reuse drips for multiple patients."

"You used to?"

"Sadly, there was a time, yes. If you don't have funds—"

"But diseases, like HIV?"

"That's why it stopped."

"Would the nurse have reused the drips?"

"I've had reports of nurses reusing devices, then charging patients for the new ones for their own profit. But that was at other hospitals."

"These things should be free."

"Theoretically. But this is Zim. People do what they have to, to survive."

"So, you think there is a possibility of that?"

"I don't think so. We implemented strict measures here, because we often get foreign tourists, and management didn't want to get sued over reckless conduct. We have a tracking system for any new equipment used, needles, syringes, drip packaging used. Packages used equal the number of patients and days in hospital. Every disposed item is also scanned again by a third party daily as an extra precaution, so it would be hard for one person to manipulate the system unless it is a collaboration."

"Food?"

"Same deal. The lab checked the food remains. Nothing unusual."

"So if it was not an employee, the only other option is the officer at the door."

"There were no signs of struggle."

"These guys are good. They're literally throwing the middle finger in our face. Not even hiding their trail. They are just flexing their muscle, showing they can outsmart us, slow us down. They knew by now we probably figured out how Conwell died."

"And this time they used the same drug, so we would find the cause of death quickly."

FIFTY-SIX

SIX'S EYES BLINKED RAPIDLY. The bright white light.

"How did I get here?"

"You drowned."

Six nodded.

"Don't talk. Lie still," Reggie said. "It's a miracle you survived."

"I don't remember anything."

"But hey, we did it," she said. "The kids are safe, all returned to their families."

"That's good."

"Jadin told me what you did. That was super brave."

Six smiled, then winced. "Never thought I would hear those words from you."

Reggie laughed. "Now you have."

"It's nothing. I knew the kid could do it."

"And the Bileses wanted you to know they are extremely grateful. They got you these." Reggie pointed to the vase of assorted roses and a get-well-soon card on the nightstand.

"That's nice. Guess the old man was clean after all."

"Yes. He was telling the truth. None of the evidence ties anything to him. Turns out the kids involvement was coincidental."

"I see. Wrong place, wrong time." Six squirmed pulling himself up to the headboard.

"Glad all the folklore worked and still led us to the kids. You must be a believer now."

"I didn't say that."

"Well, the face tells more than words."

"You can't be too sure. Some things are better left alone. Have you talked to the kids?"

"Once they were fed, they were all fine. Their families are grateful. They said the minister and the mayor decided they were not worth ransoming and too old to sell, and were keeping them as food for the creature.

"Apparently, the minister was so into the blood sacrifice thing. That was part of the ritual."

A nurse entered. "Good news, Mr. Sixpence," said the nurse. "You're cleared to leave this afternoon. She said you only have a ribcage fracture, and contusion."

"Doesn't sound too bad. Thank goodness. Can't stand the food in here."

"It's not that bad," said the nurse.

"I'm not a foodie, but man, looks like they just take everything frozen and nuke it in the microwave. My indiscriminate palate can tell that for sure. It's terrible."

Reggie yawned.

"How long have you been sitting there?"

"About eighteen hours."

"Reggie, you need to sleep," Six said.

"I know. Just wanted to make sure you were okay." A tear cascaded down her cheek. "I thought I had lost you."

"Thanks Reggie. I'm okay now."

Reggie wiped the tear and held Six's hand.

"What's wrong?" Six said.

"Clive is dead," Reggie said.

"What? He was better last time I saw him."

"Joyce says he was poisoned with the same drug concoction as Louis."

"Shit!"

"They still don't know who did it."

"The officers guarding the room?"

"I requested backup. They are being questioned as we speak."

Six pulled himself up and leaned on the headboard.

"That's why you stayed here the whole time, isn't it?"

Reggie nodded, avoiding Six's gaze.

"We were right about the meeting site," she said. "We arrested five people at the site. They all came with money and started arguing about which one won the auction."

"Do we know any of them?"

"The mayor was one. Several businessmen across Africa."

"I knew it."

Lin came in a few minutes later, one arm strapped in a sling. She handed a copy of *The*

Wall Street Journal to Reggie. "We did it, guys!" she said, smiling. "How's my boy?"

"Still hurting like hell," Six said.

"You are Superman," she said. "You will be okay."

"I wish it was as easy as you say it. This body is still flesh and bone."

"I know you will be fine," Lin said.

"Reggie, what's the news?" Six said, turning to Reggie.

"This is nuts!" Reggie said.

The news story listed several corrupt leaders who had been implicated, including a band of businessmen, oligarchs to be tried for trafficking and organized crime by the International Court, including the Nigerian and Congo ministers of mining. Several members had been rooted out of the organized crime ring, which had members in Libya, Nigeria, and Congo.

The minister had allegedly diverted over $100 million from the Chinese contractor, and other diamond and platinum mining investments. The contract gave them exclusive prospecting rights for minerals in the region, particularly lithium.

"Of course. With more electric cars on the road, lithium is the new gold," Six said.

"Electronic chips, batteries for smartphones, computers, electric vehicles."

"Everyone in Africa having wireless access, that's over two billion new users added to the demand for batteries. They can't depend on Chile and Argentina for lithium. The guys wanted local lithium sources," Lin said.

"Well, looks as if that won't happen," Reggie said.

"For now," Six said.

"The major contractor was facing a hundred-million-dollar fine for kickbacks. The city mayor and police chief were arrested on counts of corruption and kickbacks for contracts. Two officers have confessed to coercion from the police chief to poison Clive in the hospital," said Lin. "That's the local news."

"And Hellstrom?"

"The narrative is he died of a stroke," Lin said. "Using the information we confiscated, the MI6 has been able to freeze most of his assets. It will take some time to get all of his stuff."

"Man, talk about a clean slate," Reggie said. "They will have to bring in a new police chief from out of town. I know their candidate. He's known as a hothead, so his team will not mess around."

"And you?" Six said to Reggie.

"My boss said I can spend more time here until things are stable."

"Is that a good thing?"

"Of course. Who would hate a place like this? What about you?"

Six looked in the distance. "Heading back tomorrow."

"And the *Nyaminyami*?" Lin said.

"Some things are better left alone."

Six was released later that day. Because of the cracked rib, the doctor cautioned Six to avoid any physical contact. Otherwise, Six was fine. They had pumped him with fluids, solutes, and blood to replenish what he had lost.

"When are you flying out?" he asked Lin later, by phone.

"This afternoon," Lin said. "My job here is done. Superiors want me back in London."

THEY REACHED the Victoria Falls International Airport at 6 p.m. Because Six was too sore to do it, Reggie helped Lin out of the Jeep, carrying her baggage to the check-in booth.

"Surprised the big guys didn't send you a private jet."

Lin smiled. "I'm a simple girl, remember? All the flying solo M.O. scares the hell out of me. Plus, they could use that fuel money for my single trip to pay for a thousand kids here to go to school for an entire year."

"I get that."

Six slapped Lin on the shoulder.

"Ouch!" she yelped, holding the arm strapped across her chest. "Take it easy, big guy. Are you trying to destroy my arm?"

"Oh no, sorry. I didn't mean to."

"Come here," Lin said, beckoning to Reggie with her free hand.

She hugged Reggie.

"I will miss you guys."

"We will miss you too!"

Lin held back tears. "Reggie, thanks for being a good sport."

"That was one hell of a ride."

"I know. One for the ages."

"Keep in touch."

"I will. If not, I can always find you."

"Creepy!"

The two women laughed.

"Take care of yourself," Reggie said.

"You too, partner," Lin said.

Lin again hugged both Reggie and, very carefully, Six. She pulled her carry-on suitcase onto the security check conveyor belt. They waved at Lin before she disappeared behind throngs of other passengers.

SIX AND REGGIE sat in the Jeep outside of her bed-and-breakfast. Six had insisted he could drive.

"What now?"

"What does that mean?"

"I mean, what do we do now?"

"Go back to work."

"Is it that easy?"

"No, but that's all we can do. I'd rather do that than worry too much."

"You ever been to the Eastern Highlands?"

"That place known for juju, witchcraft, and necromancers and all?"

"That too. But it doesn't really exist. It's all legend."

"I see. What can we do in the Eastern Highlands?"

"We could hike Mount Inyanga!"

"Hmm!"

"Or visit Chirinda Forest, and the Big Tree!"

"That sounds fun. Then you go back to America."

"And maybe at some point you can come see my hometown in Oklahoma City."

"I'll have to think about that."

"You will?"

"Of course."

Reggie leaned in. Six inched closer. Before long, their lips locked. They held on for a little longer, as if seeking each other's permission. Six pulled back.

Six hesitated, then said, "I'm sorry. I shouldn't have done that." He started the car. "Let's forget it happened."

"Are you intimidated? I intimidate most guys."

"I can see that. But I like you. I like you a lot."

"So?"

"I feel like if I'm going to do this, I have to do this the right way."

"I didn't expect to hear that from a hunk like you. Taking things slow? I've seen the way women swoon on you in the streets, even at the station."

"Well, blame my parents for that. Guys do the same for you."

She simpered. "And you flirt with all of them."

"Does it look like that?"

"Duh, yeah."

"Well, some of us were raised by our mothers to be gentlemen. I'm a nice person and it doesn't mean I'm flirting with them. Plus, I know what I want now."

"And what is that?"

"A high-value woman."

"And?"

"Someone like you."

"How do you know? We have only known each other for a week."

"I know. But my line of work has allowed me to be a good judge of character. The way you remained stoic under pressure, your search for the truth, the way you cared about the victims, I'd say you handle stress better than I do."

"Thanks."

"There is something special about you."

"Go on. I'm listening."

"You've this kick-ass mentality that I definitely wouldn't want to mess with, yet you also exude so much feminine energy that, I'm sure, like most guys, I can't help myself. That's rare nowadays with all this push for women to be men. You balance being a boss lady and being a lady perfectly."

She smiled. "That's sweet. But I like it," she said, twirling a finger in her hair. She leaned slightly to the side, meeting Six's gaze. "I like it a lot."

"Me too."

He pulled her to him and kissed her, this

time a little longer. They locked eyes while he held her.

"I guess that's a yes you're coming to the Eastern Highlands?"

"Maybe!"

"I have your number."

"I know."

Six walked around to open the car door for Reggie.

"Man, you're about to mess up my plans," he said.

"Am I?"

"I guess I will take the chance."

Reggie smiled at him. He smiled back, seeing the brightness in Reggie he hadn't seen before. He wanted to stay one more day. She was different. And he liked it.

He backed up the car and drove towards the Safari Club.

THEY DROVE in silence for a while. Six parked the car in front of the Safari Club.

"You know," said Six, uncinching his seat belt. "Every time I send a bad guy to prison, or kill one, instead of being happy I've this sadness that I've just opened a vacant spot for another to take the reins," he said.

"I understand you completely!"

"There will always be another bad guy. And we will kill them all!"

"We, huh?" she said, gazing at Six.

"Yes. Why not? I think we make a pretty convincingly good team."

"That's a little presumptuous."

"You don't think so? Look what we have done in a week."

"We do make a pretty good team."

"Wait, did you think this was the end?"

"Now it's over, you've to fly back to the States. There's no reason for you to stick around."

"Maybe you can come visit me in the Eastern Highlands. See my grandmother. I know you two will get along."

"What makes you think that?"

"She's a badass!"

They laughed.

"Aren't you supposed to keep family private in your job?"

"Well, not for people I love—I mean trust!"

She looked at him gazing at her.

"But settling is not for people like us!" Six said.

"Is that you speaking, or your fear of attachment speaking?" she said.

"Maybe both."

"Have you tried?"

"Let's just say I've had my fair share of being burned," Six said.

"So, you gave up on it?"

"No. I just don't make it a priority now. I don't see the value in trying."

"There's so much more to life than this, you know."

"I know. But so far, I think I'm doing my fair share in making this hellhole safer. At least I think so," Six said.

"Buying some time until another douchebag comes along!"

"There'll always be one. And I'll keep putting them in body bags."

"Till when?"

"Till my time is up. Which literally is anytime, really."

"You had better enjoy every moment, then."

"That's right. Where to?"

"How about your hotel room?"

"Let's go."

They devoured each other like hungry hyenas.

FIFTY-EIGHT

SIX BOUGHT some bananas and sugarcane and walked towards the sports grounds. It felt good being back in the Eastern Highlands of the country. The weather was muggy, with dark gray angry clouds colliding in the sky. Six hoped it wouldn't rain. But that's just how it was here. One minute it's sunny, the next it's pouring.

He took out his phone and called Professor de Klerk. He explained what had happened. When he had finished, the professor sighed. Six could tell the man was sobbing.

"Thank goodness. I'll die in peace. My work was not in vain after all."

"Take care of yourself, Professor."

"Thank you. Oh. Thank you so much."

Six stood at a distance watching the kids dance in the running water at the school. They took turns pumping the borehole. He watched as the new borehole and running water pipes were installed. All from an anonymous donor. The environmental science building with empty windows was being refurbished. A dozen solar panels were being installed while ground was broken for a few more buildings for kids who learned under the trees. He sat on the embankment watching the soccer game, as the home team, dubbed the "New Brooms," played a rival school with their new kit: new jerseys and new cleats. A netball game on the adjacent patch was the "Lady New Brooms." All smiles. He smiled. *They deserve it. It's their money in the first place, anyway.*

Circumstances were hard, but Six had learned to respect their ways. Having spent some time with his grandmother, he knew things just were. Good in their own ways. Everyone looked happy, smiling, despite seeming to have nothing. Kids in ragged clothes, unkempt—but they all had genuine smiles. That was something he had not seen in the West. Only outsiders felt sorry for them, and it only felt bad when outsiders came in. All the aid and whatnot had done nothing to make this region better. And Six doubted it helped anyone apart for the press, which benefited from perpetuating a narrative of helplessness. He knew these people would fare well on their own without some savior coming in to help them. The people here had learned to hustle, to strive in the years of colonialism, dictatorship, cyclones, droughts, and hyperinflation. He knew they could build their own country if left alone.

If only that were possible. An ideal not realizable in this world.

"You did it, didn't you?"

Six turned around to see his grandmother. She set down her basket full of bananas.

"Grandma, what are you doing here?"

"I would not miss this day. That's how you make money, on sports days."

"But you don't have to make any money."

"But I want to," she said. "What should I do? Stay at home and go insane."

"What can I do to change your mind?"

"Nothing. I'm happy doing this."

"Okay, Grandma, but you know you can always stop when you want to."

"I won't. I like work."

Six rubbed her back. He smiled. She had insisted on living in her small village no matter how Six tried. He sent money now and then, but had learned the cost of Black Tax—often finding himself supporting cousins of cousins for different propositions. At times he liked it, other times he hated it, especially when others took advantage of him.

"Mothers can tell. You've a good heart. Thank you for all you did for us and all these kids." She stood. "I'll be at the market if you're staying."

Six remained quiet. *Was I really a good man? I guess only God can judge.* He watched Grandma Grace limp on with the overloaded basket.

The feeling never got old. He stopped an out-of-bounds ball and kicked it back for a throw-in.

His device beeped. It was a message.

Houston at 20:00 tomorrow.

He knew what to do. Details of his itinerary arrived shortly after. Six faded into the joyous crowds as the local high-school team, the New Brooms, scored.

AUTHOR'S NOTE

I hope you enjoyed 'The Smoke That Thunders'. As always, if you enjoyed this book, a review would be much appreciated as it helps other readers discover the story.

Sign up at jmanyanga.com to be notified of giveaways, new releases, and updates as we journey through this epic journey of discovery together.

ALSO BY J.M. MANYANGA

AORATOSIA: Invisible Within

The Declaration: A Six Thriller

MORE ADVENTURES

The character SIX emerged from observations by the author through travels around the world. J.M. Manyanga believes every person he encounters and every place he visits has a story, and that we can all do better if we are careful enough to look. Follow him on social media for updates on upcoming SIX adventures.